THIRD AND GOAL

In *First and Ten*, the opening book in this exciting series about American Football, we met the English schoolboy, Dave Sheppard, his family and his best friend, Wilburn Thomas. Though he came from a soccer-mad family, Dave gradually lost interest, being won away by the Gridiron game. Encouraged by his Uncle Don, who'd worked and lived in San Francisco, both boys joined a local youth team run by Tom Nickleby.

In *Second and Five*, set just over a year later, we saw how Dave's involvement with American Football was harming his work at school and what steps were taken to try and remedy that situation. It was a difficult time for the whole Sheppard family. On top of all the other problems, Wilburn suffered at the hands of a couple of local bullies. Since the dramatic ending to the second book in the series, only a couple of weeks have passed.

Laurence and Matthew James

★★★★★★★★★★★★★★★★★★★★★

THIRD
AND
GOAL

★★★★★★★★★★★★★★★★★★★★★

A Magnet Book

This is dedicated to Joe Montana and the
San Francisco Forty-Niners and to L.T. and
the New York Giants for all the excitement
and pleasure that they've given us and for
demonstrating that courage is, indeed,
grace under pressure. With our thanks.

First published as a Magnet original 1987
by Methuen Children's Books Ltd
11 New Fetter Lane, London EC4P 4EE
Copyright © 1987 Laurence James
Printed in Great Britain
by Richard Clay Ltd, Bungay, Suffolk

British Library Cataloguing in Publication Data

James, Lawrence
    Third and goal. – (A Gridiron story).
    – (A Magnet book).
    I. Title   II. James, Matthew   III. Series
    823'.914 [J]   PZ7

ISBN 0-416-02492-0

1 Dave Sheppard woke with a start, feeling his stomach lurch. He realised suddenly that the note of the jet engines had altered, slowing, and the jumbo seemed to be dropping downwards. For a moment he felt a wave of fright, staring intently out of the window.

'Starting the approach towards landing, Dave,' said the reassuring voice of Uncle Don, sitting in the seat next to him.

Immediately there was the hiss of the cabin intercom being switched on. 'Good afternoon, ladies and gentlemen. This is Captain Keaton here again. Just to let you know that we have begun our descent towards San Francisco International Airport. Our estimated time of arrival is six forty-five, Pacific Time. Ground temperature is sixty-seven degrees and the forecast is bright and dry.'

Dave looked down from his seat on the left side of the big aircraft, just in front of the wing. His legs felt a bit cramped from the long flight across the continent from New York, coming on top of the transatlantic hop from Heathrow to Kennedy Airport. He'd remembered Uncle Don's warning about getting dried out. 'Dehydrated' had been the word. Uncle Don had flown to and from America a lot of times in the last few years, because of his job working for Holiday Inn hotels all over the world as a relief assistant manager. 'Drink lots of Coke or Seven-Up,' he'd urged Dave. 'And don't eat too much.'

Dave peered at his watch. Uncle Don had also warned him about all the time zones they'd be passing through, going back an hour each time. Now it was nearly seven in the evening. That was the time down there, in amongst the grey and orange mountains that he could just make out through the tattered wisps of grey cloud. But his body seemed much more tired than he'd expected.

'What time is it really?' he asked his uncle.

'I can never figure it out. I get confused as well, Dave. We left home this morning about seven, didn't we? Got to Heathrow about nine. Checked in. Got some books and mags to read. Took off around ten. Then we had the wait in New York. I suppose it must be about two or three in the morning, body-time.'

Dave shook his head. 'That's really thin. No wonder I feel tired.'

'We'll go straight to my place from the airport. Clearing immigration always takes a little time. Should be away from the airport by around half-seven. There's a car waiting for us there. Say about an hour to get in to my apartment and then straight to bed for both of us. How's that sound?'

'Good.'

During the flights, Dave had noticed that his Uncle Don's English accent was already weakening and bits of American were creeping in. He said 'apartment' and not 'flat'. He'd ordered some wine with his meal. But he'd asked for a 'hafi' bottle, not a 'half'.

One of the stewardesses appeared at their row, smiling at Dave, which made him blush a bit, but he hoped she hadn't noticed.

'Won't be long now,' she said, smiling and showing the most perfect set of teeth that Dave had ever seen. 'This your first trip here?'

'Yes, it is.'

Uncle Don smiled up at the stewardess, his American accent, Dave noticed, becoming even more pronounced. 'This is my nephew, David. I work here, down at the Holiday Inn on Fisherman's Wharf.'

'I know it,' the girl said.

'Sure. Bringing young Dave here over to show him the city.'

'Enjoyed your flight with TWA today?' she asked.

'Yes. I was sort of worried about flying, but it's been great. Didn't like the feeling much when we took off. Bein' pushed back in your seat. But it's been brill.'

But she was more interested in Uncle Don. 'Gee, the way the little boy talks is really neat. I love to hear an English accent from children.'

Dave wasn't at all pleased with the 'little boy' bit.

'I'm from England, originally,' said Uncle Don, his accent getting broader and broader.

'I'd hardly notice. But the little boy . . . He's been drinking so much Coke that I was kind of worried that he might float away on it,' she said, with just a touch of a reproach.

Uncle Don heard it in her voice and responded. 'I told him to drink plenty of soft drinks. Stop him dehydrating and feeling more jet-lagged.'

'Sure,' she said, smiling brightly at both of them and moving on down the aisle, making sure that people were doing up their seat-belts, ready for the landing. As the plane tilted to the left, Dave got a great view out over the city of San Francisco, seeing the silvery sheen of water on both sides of the peninsula where it stood.

'We may get a chance to see . . .' began Uncle Don, bringing his seat back to the upright position.

But the intercom interrupted him once more. 'Captain Keaton here again. Just a note for you sports buffs on our flight who're sitting on the left side of the aircraft. Down there you can seen the green shape of Candlestick Park, home of the San Francisco baseball team, the Giants.' He paused, Dave waiting eagerly. 'And, of course, the home field for the San Francisco Forty-Niners.'

To Dave's delight, from several seats around him he heard passengers cheering the mention of the Forty-Niners. His favourite team.

And there it was. Sticking out into the glittering waters of the San Francisco Bay, like a stubby thumb of land, the emerald of the pitch like a bright beacon. By now the plane had come down so low that the baseball diamond was clearly visible. Dave wished that they'd been flying in on a Sunday evening in winter, so that he could have seen the floodlights and the crowds and the gridiron pattern on the turf. Maybe even have made out the tiny scarlet figures of the players.

Uncle Don was leaning over him, peering down, his

8

arm on Dave's shoulder. 'Boy, I'm coming home,' he said.

'If only it could have been during the football season,' Dave said, quietly.

'Yeah. Be good. Maybe some other time, Dave. They'll all be up at their training camp this time of year.'

Dave knew about training camps. Every year, in the middle of summer, all the National Football League teams held them. Their regular squad got together for the beginning of fitness and tactics training. But it was also the time that the hopefuls turned up. Young men from all over who thought they could become quarterbacks, or receivers or tackles or kickers, or whatever. Often hundreds would be there, attracted by the lure of joining the Forty-Niners or the Dolphins or the Giants. And of those hundreds, one or two might eventually make it to the starting squad. The opposite side of the same coin was that the players from the previous season would also have to prove to the coaches that they were still good enough to make it. The tensions, Dave knew, during the pre-season camps were often enormous, with older players finally being cut, and the occasional young hopeful coming through to success.

'Don't suppose we could go up there, could we, Uncle Don?'

'I've told you before. Cut out the "uncle" bit. Makes me feel ninety. Go to training camp? Doubt it. Like I said when I asked you if you wanted to come, I'm goin' to be real busy at work a lot of the time. But I guess I'll find a few hours to show you round.'

'Not their camp? Is it too far?'

'Kind of. Not in the city. Sierra Community College, out at Rocklin. About a hundred miles northeast of San Francisco, through Sacramento, out on Interstate Eighty. Got to be around a five hour drive there and back.'

'Oh, I see,' said Dave, trying to hide his disappointment. Though he was desperately excited at coming to America like this, he was a touch sad that he'd be in San Francisco for a fortnight or so and not get to see anything of the Forty-Niners.

The plane swooped lower and lower, until Dave could make out individual houses, and cars snaking sedately along winding roads. Tiny rectangles of turquoise in many of the back gardens proved his belief that every house in America had its own swimming-pool. His ears popped and he swallowed hard to clear them, like Uncle Don had recommended him to do.

The man in the seat next to Uncle Don was still bent over his pocket calculator, stabbing at the buttons, muttering to himself and making notes on a snakeskin pad. He'd introduced himself to them both within about thirty seconds of taking off from Heathrow. His name was Andy Zentner and he came from Corte Madera, just across the Golden Gate Bridge from San Francisco. He announced that he was a realtor who'd moved out west from Marathon, Texas some years back. Uncle Don had whispered later that a realtor was like an estate agent. Andy had a dark-haired wife and three teenage children. He showed them the pictures from a capacious wallet. He also

10

gave Uncle Don his business card and scribbled his home address on it. 'Y'all come see me some time, you hear?' he'd said. Dave wondered if all Americans were going to be that friendly.

Andy had also been a Forty-Niners man and he and Uncle Don spent a fair part of the flight from London to New York locked in talk about the team. Dave listened eagerly, occasionally being able to add something from his own store of knowledge. While they waited at Kennedy Airport to change planes, Andy had gone off, explaining he had some business calls to make. But he'd managed to get the seat next to them for the second part of the trip as well.

Dave felt his stomach jump again as the jumbo made its final descent into the airport, which was also sticking out into the edge of the Bay. There was the faintest bump and a distant screech of rubber as the tyres kissed the runway, and they were down. He looked into his lap and found his fingers all tangled up round each other, his knuckles white.

But they were down. He was there.

Immigration and customs passed in a haze. Uncle Don took charge of everything, knowing where to go and when, like the seasoned traveller he was. All Dave remembered was the man at the immigration desk asking him where he was staying and when he was going back. He wasn't exactly unfriendly, but he didn't make Dave feel very welcome.

The car was ready and waiting once they got outside. It was warm and the skies were blue as they stepped outside the terminal building, Dave carrying

11

his small suitcase. When they'd changed planes at New York, the temperature had been in the upper eighties, and even in the airport it felt uncomfortably sticky. Here the air was fresher and cleaner.

'Tired?'

Dave nodded. 'Yes. I feel a bit weird, really.'

'That's jet-lag. Like being a touch the worse for drink, Dave. Don't worry. Get back to my place and have a quick snack. Then straight to bed. Feel right as rain in the morning. Sleep in, if you like. It's a Sunday. Haven't got to be at work, so we can both relax.'

They pulled out of the car-park, on to a road marked 'Highway 101'. And instantly, Dave felt that he'd slipped into the middle of an American film, or television programme. Driving on the right, with all the billboards and cars seeming both ridiculously alien, yet totally familiar to him.

Uncle Don reached down and switched on the radio. It was some sort of phone-in, with people criticising something called 'zoning'. It sounded interesting at first, then Dave realised it was like planning permission for where you could build new houses. Uncle Don got bored with it and eventually found a station playing rock music.

'Blast from the past time. A rave from the grave. A genuine solid golden zoom from the tomb from the sultans of swing. Dire Straits with 'Romeo And Juliet'. The time here in San Francisco is eight minutes short of the hour of eight o'clock on Saturday August third. Temperature is in the low sixties. Forecast for the remainder of the weekend for the Bay area is mainly sunny with an afternoon high of seventy-four and only a five per cent chance of precipitation. Winds from the north. Have a great evening with the ones you love. Enjoy this. Dire Straits.'

It was one of Dave's favourites, from an earlier album. There was a momentary wave of homesickness that he managed to quell. Swallowing hard to clear his emotion, he looked around them.

A hillside to the right was covered with little white boxes, spread and neat. Each house slightly different from the one next to it. They crossed over a causeway, and then Dave's heart leaped. Seeing a road-sign that pointed the turning for Candlestick Park. To be so near . . .

The light was fading. Away to his far left, in the distance, he saw what looked like great rolling mountains of grey and white.

'What's that, Don?' he asked.

'Where? Oh, that. Fog, Dave. San Francisco, 'cos of where it's situated, gets a lot of fog coming in off of the sea. Most evenings you get to see that. Spectacular, isn't it?'

It was. But now they were close to the city, the traffic becoming heavier. Taxis and single-decker buses lumbering and roaring past them. Signs came and went on both sides of the road, to parts of the city that he'd never heard of. The road forked, part of the traffic going off towards the Oakland Bay Bridge, but they looped up and round, heading towards Uncle Don's flat.

'Apartment,' said Dave, to himself. Determined he'd try to avoid any obvious Englishisms while he was there. Dad had given him a little paperback book with equivalent words in it for America and England. He'd studied it on the way over with TWA, in between meals and glasses of soft drinks.

'How far?'

Dave found his ears were still popping, and when Uncle Don spoke, it sounded muffled, and somehow unreal. Maybe that was part of jet-lag as well.

'Near the corner of Chestnut and Leavenworth Streets. Close by that very winding street I told you about. Remember that photo of it?'

'Lampard Street, was it called?'

'Lombard Street, Dave. It's only a short walk from the Holiday Inn where I'll be working. Place belongs to a friend of mine called Mark Howell. Works in publishing. But he's over in Europe for a few weeks and he's lent it to me. Two bedrooms on the second floor.'

'What we call the first floor, Don,' said Dave, proud he'd remembered that through the fog that was settling over San Francisco and over his brain as tiredness raced nearer.

He started to drop off to sleep in the car, lulled by the quiet music and the humming of the engine. Once he woke up and there was water on his right, with some docks and jetties. Once he thought he saw a very tall, skinny black man wearing red satin shorts and a white tee-shirt. Riding a one-wheeled cycle, weaving and turning through the traffic. But he decided he must have dreamed it.

Then Uncle Don was shaking him by the arm. The

car had stopped at a steep angle, and it was full night outside.

'We're there, Dave.'

His tongue felt too big for his mouth, and it seemed like it was made from cotton-wool. When he got out he staggered at the steepness of the hill. Far worse than anything he'd ever seen. There was a sharp slope in Bishop's Stortford, back near home, where he sometimes went shopping with his mother. But it was nothing like this. It was like standing on the side of a mountain.

'Careful,' said his uncle.

There was a sign by the car which said 'Prevent Runaways. Curb wheels and engage gear.'

'I'll rustle up some grub for us,' said Uncle Don. 'Want to go in and put your stuff away? Take the room at the back. It's quieter.'

Dave went in, seeing a single bed, against a wall. The curtains were pulled shut and the apartment smelled stuffy, as though it hadn't been open for several days.

The bed looked extremely inviting and he decided to just lie down on it for a few minutes, until the food was ready.

Dave lay down, and closed his eyes for a moment.

'Breakfast's ready, Dave. Come on, you can't sleep all day.'

★★★★★★ The sun was streaming in through the large windows of the apartment. Dave stood up, shaking his head to try and clear away the cobwebs of the long flight from England. Already he'd lost track of what time his body thought it was. The clock on the chest of drawers in his bedroom said nine fifteen. He concentrated a moment.

'Eight hours. Means it's about five in the afternoon back home.'

He could smell fresh coffee and bacon frying. Just for a few seconds he sat on his bed and allowed himself a pang of isolation. He was thousands and thousands of miles from his family. From Eastbury. From 66, Dower Street. His own room and records and possessions. From Mum and Dad. From his older brothers, Danny, Jimmy and Alan and his sister, Carol. She'd given him her favourite lucky gonk to carry. A little plastic dwarf, about four inches high, with long purple hair. He'd packed it carefully in one of his spare pair of trainers.

Dave also thought about his best friend, Wilburn Thomas. Wilburn was the wide receiver for the Downham Destroyers, the youth gridiron team that Dave played quarterback for. The played very well together, and they'd helped take the Destroyers to the top of their league, winning the area cup.

'Come on, you little slugabed.'

'Coming.'

Only then did it strike him that he was wearing just a Blues Brothers tee-shirt and pants. Uncle Don must have undressed him and put him to bed. Dave felt terribly embarrassed at that. Nobody had put him to bed since he was about three years old. Ten years ago.

He quickly pulled on his jeans, considering whether to open his case for clean socks. Deciding not to bother, he picked up yesterday's pair and tugged them on, tying his dark blue Pony linebacker trainers. He went out of his bedroom, passing a long mirror on the wall. Pausing and straightening his hair.

'Checking the reflec?' teased Uncle Don.

'Yes. Sorry 'bout crashing out like that, last night, Uncle . . . Don. Must have been more tired than I thought. Sorry.'

Uncle Don laughed. 'Don't worry. Jet-lag's worse when you fly back home to England, so be prepared. I remember slumping face down in a plate of spaghetti once when I got home. Here's breakfast.'

Dave was ravenously hungry.

There was fresh chilled orange juice for starters, followed by some strips of crispy bacon, with a couple of fried eggs. 'They're over easy,' said Uncle Don. 'Means they're fried both sides. Do them one side like your mother does and that's called sunnyside.'

'What's this?' asked Dave, pointing his fork at some peculiar looking fried vegetable on the side of his plate. He peered cautiously at it, deciding it seemed like shredded potato.

'They're hash browns. Try it. You'll love them, Dave.'

'But what are they?'

'Oh. Shredded potato, fried.'

Dave took some, dipping them in the golden yolk of the egg. His uncle was right. They were absolutely delicious. The bacon tasted a bit odd; not quite like English bacon. The toast was wholewheat with some sort of low-cal margarine.

'Jelly?'

'Sorry?'

'Do you want some jelly with your toast, Dave? There's blueberry and loganberry.'

Dave remembered. Jelly was jam and jello was jelly. 'I'll try blueberry, please, Don.'

'You're welcome.'

His father's brother was becoming more and more American with every passing hour. Somehow the clothes Uncle Don was wearing, which had seemed a bit bizarre in England, now looked just right.

'Coffee?'

'White with three sugars, please.'

'You want to run that past me again, Dave?'

'Oh, yeah. I mean "with", don't I?'

'That's better. Ask for it white or black and you'll throw the waitress.'

He took the glass jug from its stand and poured out a big white mug of coffee. There was cream on the table and a bowl of brown sugar. Dave helped himself.

'My friend Mark's a health freak. Works out with weights and swims a lot. On a good day he can crack walnuts with his eyelashes,' said Uncle Don, sitting

18

down opposite Dave. 'That's why there's a whole lot of brown rice and spun soya and vegetables here. I'm more of a junk-food man when I'm home. We can buy some stuff at the deli on the corner. That's like a grocery shop in England, but with a bigger range of foods.'

Dave wiped his plate with another slice of the brown bread. Back home they generally ate white sliced, but this didn't taste bad at all. He sipped at the coffee, looking across the sunlit room, hearing traffic go by. It was *American* traffic. He was in San Francisco. David Sheppard from Eastbury, on the borders of Essex and Hertfordshire, was sitting having breakfast in San Francisco.

Home of the Forty-Niners.

Sunday passed in a haze of unique memories and mixed impressions. Uncle Don knew the city of San Francisco very well and took his nephew on a racing tourists' eye-view of the place.

It was wonderful.

The sun shone the whole day and the air tasted fresh and salty. Since the city was also a fishing port, it wasn't surprising that Dave found he could catch the faintest hint of the sea wherever they went.

They walked down Chestnut, and turned left along Columbus Avenue. Dave asked if they could go into a huge branch of Tower Records. Uncle Don agreed but warned him about spending too much money so early in the holiday. He also reminded Dave that he had promised to send a card to his family today. They slipped into the lobby of the Holiday Inn, on the edge of Fisherman's Wharf, where Don Sheppard would be working for the next few months. He went off to report to the manager, leaving Dave to browse through the small gift shop. There were lots of free brochures of things to see and do around the city and he helped himself to several of them, thinking they'd make good souvenirs to show his parents and Wilburn.

'We have to ride the tramcars.' said Uncle Don when he came out. 'We'll walk down to the Wharf and look at the Bay and the Bridge. Tour the shops and then get a tramcar near Ghirardelli Square, up towards Chinatown. Grab some food there and then walk on back here. How does that sound?'

'Fine.'

'Then let's do it.'

If it hadn't been for Uncle Don's warning about saving some cash, Dave could easily have blown his whole fortnight's allowance that first Sunday morning.

Every shop they went into seemed to have wonderful presents for the whole family. Great souvenirs. One place seemed to specialise in all kinds of football gifts. Posters and shirts and jackets and pennants. Dave couldn't resist a poster for Wilburn of his hero, Miami Dolphins' Number Eighty-Three, Mark Clayton, the wide receiver. There was also a range of pictures of the Forty-Niners, including posters of Dave's own hero, Joe Montana, Number Sixteen.

The Golden Gate Bridge, with its soaring, graceful arch, was just like the pictures he'd seen. Painted a reddish brown colour. 'Red for the blood of the failed country singers that come here to throw themselves off the bridge,' said Uncle Don.

'Honest?'

'No. Not really, Dave. Just a story.'

The waters of the Bay were dotted with the darting white sails of small boats, taking part in some kind of regatta. Uncle Don pointed out the settlements of Tiburon and Sausalito on the far side.

'Very trendy, that is. Expensive, with loads of little boutiques. Might go there. It's not far from there out to Muir Woods. That you have to see, Dave.'

'What's Muir Woods?'

'Kind of a park. Groves of big redwoods. Bigger than any tree you've ever seen. Magic.'

'Is that Alcatraz?' asked Dave, pointing to a long, narrow island, a mile or so out from where they stood on the dock of the Bay. The sun bounced off a range of pale buildings.

'That's it. Toughest prison in the world, they used to say. Closed years ago. Clint Eastwood made a film there.'

'Can we go?'

Uncle Don looked thoughtful. 'Mebbe, Dave. See how my work fits in with it. They do boat trips. Got to book early. They're one of the favourite tourist attractions in the city.'

People dressed so differently from home, Dave thought. Lots of light, bright colours, and shorts everywhere. There was an enormously fat man, who must have weighed around twenty-five stones, in a pair of canary-yellow shorts and a tee-shirt that must have been XXXXXXXXXL size. If he'd seen him in

England, Dave would have found the sight really awful. But somehow it didn't seem that way in San Francisco.

They went into a museum filled with pictures and models of all sorts of record-breaking things. Fattest and tallest and thinnest and most valuable. Uncle Don fell a little behind Dave so that when the boy emerged on the pavement he was on his own. He stood there, thinking 'sidewalk' to himself, drinking it all in. Right at his side there was a lifesize model of a man, made up like Charlie Chaplin, with a bowler hat at a rakish angle, moustache and bendy cane. While he waited for his uncle, Dave stood in front of the dummy, looking at the cleverly modelled features .

Then it moved!

The nose twitched, the mouth opened in a smile. The hand lifted the stick to push the bowler to the back of the curly head. And it spoke.

'Ask yourself, son, whether I'm real or whether you are. Come on, make my day.'

With a twirl of the cane the figure hopped off down the street, feet clattering on the sidewalk, shadow sharp and clear in the sunlight. All round him passers-by laughed and pointed and Dave felt utterly ridiculous. Uncle Don came out at that moment, catching the tail-end of his embarrassment. When Dave had told him what had happened, he laughed as well.

'Street theatre, Dave. City's full of guys like that. Musicians and mimes and jugglers and fire-eaters. You see them a lot out in Golden Gate Park.'

* * *

The tram-cars rattled and shook and seemed on some of the steep hills as if they were going to just fall right off the edge of the world. They were so crowded that Dave saw men and women hanging on the outside, resting calmly on the running-boards. The locals seemed amazingly casual, swinging on as the car rumbled by them, dropping off at junctions with the same ease. Dave wished he could have tried it, but Uncle Don had made sure that they got a seat inside.

'There's steel cables running under the streets and each tram has some kind of pincers, that grip it, and it's hauled along that way. To stop, the driver just releases the grip on the moving cable. Few years back there was talk of scrapping the whole lot, but you could hear the outcry clear in Oakland.'

The car bumped so much that Dave felt as though his eyes were going to be shaken from their sockets, but he still loved the ride. They passed a restaurant with a sign that he was sure said: 'Fried ice-cream. So good we had to patent it.'

How could you fry ice-cream? It would melt if you put it . . . then something else caught his eye and then another something else.

Chinatown was an area of several city blocks with lots of old buildings and narrow streets and alleys. Dave had been to Gerrard Street in London's Soho, with its Oriental shops and restaurants, but this was vastly bigger. Street signs were both in English and Chinese and he even saw a red telephone box with a layered roof, like a miniature pagoda.

'Fancy some ice-cream, Dave?'

'Please, Don.'

'We'll have a kind of snack lunch and then eat at the Holiday Inn. They do a buffet there that'll knock your eyes out.'

After the ride on the tram-car, Dave wasn't too sure he wanted his eyes adjusting a second time in the same day.

In a quiet courtyard, off one of the main streets, they passed a young couple, intent on their music. A girl with very long brown hair, playing a flute, and her male companion, with his dark hair tied back in a pony-tail, playing classical guitar.

'They buskin', Don?' asked Dave.

'Guess not. Just for the love of it. Look, there's a good place for ice-cream.'

For the umpteenth time that strange disorientating Sunday, Dave boggled at what he saw.

There must have been about a hundred different flavours. Lots of places in England you got three choices. White, brown or pink. Here there were flavours he'd never even heard of: 'Rocky Road', 'Maple and Pecan', 'Bubble-gum', 'Kiwi and Guava', 'Pina Colada', 'Peach Ripple with Walnuts', 'Coconut and Honey'.

'Well?' asked Don.

'Coconut and Honey, please,' gasped Dave.

'Single scoop, double or triple or mixed?' asked the Chinese girl behind the spotless glass counter.

'Make it a double, please, miss,' said Uncle Don.

It was huge: two great whirling pyramids of creamy wonder, streaked with darker trickles of honey. Dave took it carefully. 'Thank you very much,' he said.

'You're welcome,' she replied.

'I'll have pistachio single scoop, and a double topper of passion fruit,' said Uncle Don.

When he'd eventually finished it, Uncle Don asked Dave if he wanted anything else to eat. 'Hot dog with mustard? Burger?'

'No, thanks. I'm really stuffed.'

They walked slowly on, pausing now and again to go into any store that looked interesting. Though it was out of the football season, he saw loads of people wearing Forty-Niners badges and sweaters.

'You said about there being a sort of youth team linked to the Forty-Niners, Don?' he said, as they reached the top of one of the countless hills that made up the city.

'They call themselves the Junior Forty-Niners,' replied his uncle. 'Not sure about whether there's an official tie-in. They train several times a week during the summer vacations. Out the back of the Steinhart Aquarium, in Golden Gate Park.'

Dave decided that when they got back to the apartment he'd look up on his little folding street map where that was. He'd love to go and see how they trained.

'Tomorrow I'll get my friend Ray Haffkine to take you over there. His son plays and he helps with the offense coaching.'

'Really? That'd be . . .'

'Brill?' said Uncle Don.

'Très bon, Don,' joked Dave.

By around four o'clock, Dave was finding the jet-lag creeping up on him again. His excitement at being in

25

San Francisco kept him going, despite the endless hills. But each hill brought its own view across different parts of the city, sometimes the Bay and the bridges, sometimes the business section of the city. Dave grinned in recognition at the famous building he'd seen in so many pictures. The triangular Trans-America tower, tapering down to a fine needle of white concrete.

All round the city he knew what the time was from the changing clocks on many buildings, showing both the time and the temperature. 'Three fifty-seven. Sixty-nine degrees.'

'Not far to Russian Hill, Dave,' said his uncle, encouraging.

'That what they call the place where we're staying?'

'Sure is. Tell you what. We'll stop off some place and get us some cards. You gotta write home tonight. Have a rest and then go eat. Then early to bed. Big day for both of us tomorrow.'

'Dear Mum and Dad and all at home. Planes were thin. Flew over Winsor Castle. Met man who was fan of 49ers. Don's appartment is nice. Food good. Lovely ice-cream. Seen Golden Gate Bridge and fog. China-town. Flew over Candlestick Park. Going to youth team tomorrow. Weather's good but foggy. Only evening.' As an afterthought he added: 'Missing you all', and signed his name to it.

Then he remembered something his mother had been concerned about. He took up the felt-tip again, squeezing in another line at the bottom of the card: 'PS We got a washing-machine here.'

Don was lying on the sofa in the living-room, watching a game-show on television. From what Dave had been able to see and hear it made 'The Price Is Right' look like a gathering of the terminally shy and retiring. One big lady with a curly blonde wig won a car and behaved as if she'd been given the keys to Paradise itself.

'Finished the cards?'

'Done the family. I'll send one to Will as well before we go and eat.'

'For sure. We'll go around six thirty.'

Dave took the completed card, with its crystal-clear photo of the Golden Gate Bridge, and went back to his own room. The card he'd bought for Wilburn was a picture of Joe Montana.

'It's brill, Will. Brill hills. Seen Candlestick Park. Great record shop. Watched some telly. Saw bit of baseball on news. Had great ice-cream. Going to youth gridiron team tomorrow. Bit nervous. Good flight. Met 49ers fan. Flew over Candlestick Park.' He realised he'd already mentioned that but he didn't bother to cross it out. 'Going to supper. See you soon. Best wishes to your mum and dad. And Errol and Jolene.'

He had to write really small to get it in. Putting down Will's address brought another sweeping wave of isolation. A bleakness at being so far away from home, with only Uncle Don to hold away utter loneliness.

'Will Thomas, 9 Sundial Grove, Eastbury, Essex, England.'

It seemed an eternity away. Yesterday morning he'd still been there.

The passing gloom lifted as Uncle Don called him to hurry up so they could go and eat supper.

Dave wished the floor would open and swallow him up. In England, waiters didn't behave like this, yelling and waving their arms.

It had started well enough.

The restaurant was really classy, Dave thought, and everyone there knew Uncle Don, greeting him with a wave, the head waiter showing them to their table in the corner. Uncle Don had mentioned there being a great buffet there, but Dave didn't honestly know what that meant, until he saw the long display table running most of one wall, groaning with all kinds of food.

'I'll have a half bottle of the Pinot Noir, and a Coke for my guest.'

'Is this your nephew David?' asked the man, grinning down in a friendly way.

'Sure is. First day in the city.'

'What do you guys think of it here?'

Dave wondered who he was talking to, then realised he just meant him. 'It's great, thanks.'

'You're welcome,' the reply now beginning to sound familiar to Dave.

'Hi. I'm your waiter, Steve, and it'll be my pleasure to serve you tonight.'

Steve was around twenty-five, tall and slender, with waved blond hair. He smiled at Don, who went again through the introductions for Dave's benefit.

'What're you going to enjoy tonight?' asked Steve.

Uncle Don had pointed out the finer points of the buffet before Steve's arrival, saying about the range of different fishes it contained.

'I'll have that fish thing,' said Dave, pointing across the restaurant.

Which was when Steve's yell of horror rang out, loud enough to shatter crystal.

'Fish thing! Fish thing !!! FISH THING!!!!!' dropping his pad and pen in his dismay. Stooping to pick them up. 'That fish thing, my young Englishman, is known as the Chef's Seafood Extravaganza and don't forget it.'

He grinned as he spoke, and Dave realised, to his own surprise, that he didn't actually feel embarrassed any longer. It was all right. Steve was just kidding him along.

'Sorry. Don said it was great.'

'Great? It's better than great. How does star-toppling and utterly apocalyptic sound, Dave? How 'bout a cornucopia of culinary concatenation?'

'Don't know what that means,' said Dave.

'Never mind 'bout knowin', son. Just go up there and load the platter high.'

Steve made a note of what they'd ordered and went off, spreading light and amusement amongst the other tables. Don watched him, grinning broadly at Dave. 'Not like the average waiter in England, huh, nephew?'

'No way.'

'Steve's great talent is that he's a terrific waiter. And he's good entertainment as well. He might insult people but he does it jokingly and everyone loves him. Gets more recommendations than any other staff member. Come on, let's go tackle that buffet.' They stood up, putting their napkins on the table. 'And don't let your eyes get too much bigger than your belly. Steve can be real hard on folks who take more'n they can eat.'

For the second, or was it third, time that day, Dave Sheppard felt so full that he feared he might burst. He'd been prepared for portions and helpings being bigger in the States than in England. But not this much bigger.

He'd asked Don about the various kinds of food in the containers in the buffet, all excellently cooked and beautifully displayed.

'Sea bass, salmon, tuna and swordfish. Lobster and crab. Oysters and abalone. Take a bit of each and see which you like best. That's rice and there's some potato salad. Little red things are cherry tomatoes. The dressings for the salad are in those tubs at the far end. Blue cheese, French and Thousand Island. Help yourself.'

'Can I take as much as I like?'

'But no dirty plates, Dave,' hissed Steve, almost in his ear. 'Chef doesn't like that.'

The meal was one of the best of Dave's life. He decided that the lobster was about his favourite and he was promptly urged by both Steve and his uncle to go and have a second helping. For afters there were delicious strawberries and peaches, with cherry cheesecake and ice-cream.

Uncle Don had a glass of a brown liqueur that smelled strongly of marzipan. He allowed Dave a sip, who found that it also tasted strongly of marzipan. They both finished off the supper with a cup of coffee. Dave remembered to say 'with' when asked by Steve.

They walked back through the quiet roads, up Chestnut Street, to the apartment. Dave thanked his uncle, who smiled at him. 'Been a lot of fun, nephew. Tomorrow I start work and you get to go see some youth gridiron. Sure you won't be bored?'

'No. I'm a bit nervous, you know. But I'm lookin' forward to it.'

He found it more difficult than the night before to get to sleep, being woken by a police siren howling past like an enraged dinosaur. But in the end the traditional dark pool opened up by his feet and he slipped into it.

★★★★★★ 'English kids are all retards!'

'What?'

The boy sneered and spat on the dry, brown turf. 'All retards. Mutants

★★★★★★ and punks.'

Dave couldn't think of anything to say in reply.

Don's friend, Ray Haffkine, had collected Dave in a beaten-up Chevvy soft-top at about ten in the morning. Uncle Don had gone off to work at eight, waking Dave and telling him to get his own breakfast, not to go out and only to open the door to Ray Haffkine, whom he described as a tall man with a black beard. He'd omitted to mention that Ray had tiny red ribbons plaited throughout the bushy growth of beard, making him look like some eighteenth century pirate chieftain.

He'd driven Dave out to the training session for the Junior Forty-Niners, pointing out places of interest as they went through the brightly sun-drenched city. Out of the side window Dave could see a peculiar tower, towards the Bay, with its top shaped like the end of a fireman's hose. He said that to Ray, who laughed.

'Absolutely top-hole, Dave, old sport,' he said in a terrible imitation of an English accent, dropping it when he saw the look of pain on the boy's face. 'Sorry. Not too good at accents, I guess. No, but you're right. That's Coit Tower. There was a girl named Lillie Hitchcock back in the mid to late eighteen hundreds. Fanatic about the San Francisco firemen. She married a guy called Ben Coit and died a very rich old lady in about nineteen thirty. Left a lot of money for that tower to be built.'

On the way to the Golden Gate Park, they passed some really beautiful old wooden houses, all neat and trim. Ray said that they were mainly from the end of last century and the beginning of this one. They were painted in different colours, dark greens, blues, pale pinks and yellows, like a row of scaled-up dolls' houses.

Ray parked the car, leading the way across some stretches of grass, along a winding path. It was a Monday morning, but the park seemed full of life. There was a group of five men, all playing saxophones, their melodies weaving through the fresh, calm air. Two girls were throwing a frisbee back and forth, making acrobatic catches, shrieking and laughing.

'Here we are,' Ray had said, pointing to a group of around fifty boys, most in training shirts and trousers. A few wore full gear, including helmets, making them look much bigger than the rest. 'What's your weight and height, Dave?' asked Ray as they strolled to join the Junior Forty-Niners.

'I'm five feet seven and I weigh about eight stone four.'

'What the . . . I gotta work it out. Eight stones and

33

four pounds . . . There's fourteen pounds to a stone, right?'

'Yes.'

'Yeah. So you weigh in at one-sixteen. Kind of light. You're thirteen.'

'And a . . .' Dave hesitated, picking the American pronunciation of the word. 'And a half.'

'For sure. Most of the guys here are fourteen. Some close to fifteen. You a quarterback?'

'Yes.'

'You good?'

Dave was foxed by that question. In England, you were generally taught to be modest and play down your own achievements. Over in the States that didn't seem to apply.

'We won the cup and the league.'

Ray clapped him on the back. 'Typically British kinda understatement, Dave. Come on and meet some of the guys here.'

In the background a massive ghetto-blaster was pumping out Springsteen's version of 'War', with a lot of the boys sitting round it. As Ray took him round, several of them waved a greeting.

'This is Chip Altman. Starting quarterback on the team. Chip, this is Dave Sheppard. Plays quarterback for a youth team back in England.'

Chip was a couple of inches taller than Dave, and looked a year older. He was wearing the red and gold playing strip, obviously modelled on the Forty-Niners', with the number sixteen on it. He shook hands with Dave, grinning at him.

34

'Hi, Dave. Good to see you. Thought you all played soccer over there.'

'Used to. Not so much now. Gridiron's taken off in a big way.'

'Which NFL team d'you support?'

'Forty-Niners, of course. I wear that playing number as well.'

'For Joe Montana. Hey, that's great. You guys!' He called to the group around the cassette-player. 'Dave here's a quarterback and he wears sixteen.'

'You got any teams over there good enough to take on an NFL team?' asked one of the squad. A tall, skinny black boy, wearing the number of a receiver.

'No way at all. It's growing fast, though. Several leagues, all sponsored. And the NFL Supporters' Club has started in England. You get all the news, badges, posters and stuff.'

A podgy, freckled boy came up and tapped Dave on the shoulder. He wore number eleven on his playing-shirt. 'You figure to be any good?'

'I don't know,' replied Dave, feeling an instinctive hostility towards this boy. He noticed that Ray Haffkine had gone over to start the team practice.

'Don't know. What a jerk!'

'Lay off him, Mike. Dave, this is Mike Pomfret who figures he's second-string quarterback. But he's like ten light years behind me.'

Pomfret raised a finger to Chip in an unpleasant gesture. 'You just get the luck, Altman.'

Dave couldn't let that go unchallenged. 'I think it was Mike Ditka, the Bears' coach, said that good teams have skill and bad teams always say they don't have luck.'

Pomfret looked at him in disgust. 'What d'you know 'bout it?'

'I learn what I can.'

'English kids are all retards!'

'What?'

The boy sneered and spat on the dry, brown turf. 'All retards. Mutants and punks.'

Dave couldn't think of anything to say in reply. Ray Haffkine had come up behind them, unseen, and had heard Mike Pomfret's comments.

'Shame you can't play offense as well as you shoot your mouth off, son,' he said, tight voice betraying his anger. 'Dave here's a guest. I want him to watch how we train. Mebbe come in with us a couple of times.'

Mike Pomfret didn't reply to the coach. Turning on his heel he walked away, shoulders set in an ill-tempered way.

'Sorry 'bout that, Dave,' apologised Chip Altman. 'He's the retard, not you.' Calling after Ray Haffkine, 'Coach!'

'Yeah, Chip?'

'If we got a good lead in the fourth quarter in the big one next week, mebbe Dave can come on for a play?'

Haffkine grinned. 'Could be. Watch and see what you can pick up, Dave. I'll give you a kind of try-out at the end of the session.'

'What's your big match, Chip?' asked Dave, feeling a pulse of excitement building. Even to go on for one

36

play with a team like this would be a great experience for him.

'Oakland Raiders.'

Dave knew the name from reference books on the gridiron game that he'd studied at home. Many loaned by Uncle Don or by his coach in England, Tom Nickleby.

'That was the name before they became the LA Raiders in about eighty-one.'

Chip whistled. 'You know your football, Dave. That's real good. This is their youth team and they didn't change the name.'

Dave had been about to say that he also knew that Tom Flores had stayed as coach when the team moved from Oakland, just across the Bay from San Francisco, to Los Angeles. But he decided that it might seem a bit like showing off.

'They your biggest rivals?'

'You could say that. You're the boy from England, aren't you?'

Dave turned round and saw a girl nearly his height, wearing a Junior Forty-Niners shirt and a very brief scarlet skirt, trimmed with white imitation fur. Her hair was bleached by the California sun until it was almost the colour of fresh-fallen snow. He noticed how blue her eyes were and how sun-tanned her arms and legs were.

'Yes. Yes, I am.'

'Hi. I'm Alix Cassady. Nice to meet you.' She shook his hand, with a firm grip. 'Be nice to talk some time. I'd love to come to England. Got to go practise now. See you around, David.'

'Yes. See you around.' Only as she trotted away did he realise that he hadn't blushed. Girls were something of a mystery to him, as they were to most of his friends.

'She's a real nice person, Dave,' said Chip. 'Her dad's a big wheel with the Forty-Niners. Something on executive management. Like the clothes?'

'Yes. She's not . . . not a cheer-leader, is she?'

'Sure. The best, Dave. She's lead leader in the squad. Most of the guys really like her. But . . .' It seemed as though there was something he wanted to say, but he was hesitating. 'Mike Pomfret, Dave. The number eleven. He sort of thinks he and Alix are . . . you know?'

'Goin' steady?'

'Yeah. But they're not. Alix doesn't go for that kind of stuff. She's closing in on fourteen. Says she won't start to date steady until she's at least fifteen. But Mike sees her as his girl. If she talks to anyone else he can get mean. Just a sort of word of warning. You don't mind?'

'Course not, Chip. Thanks.'

'Split left eighty. Let's complete this one, Chip,' called Haffkine, standing on the sideline near Dave.

The boys broke from the huddle, ready to practise the offense play. Dave had been impressed with the skill and fluid expertise that the American boys showed. Proud though he was of the achievements of his own team, the Downham Destroyers, he had to acknowledge that they wouldn't have stood a chance against the Junior Forty-Niners. Hardly any of his mates would have even got on the starting line-up over here.

He was specially impressed with Chip Altman. The boy was a born quarterback. Confident and athletic, ready to throw a pass or scramble for short yardage when the need arose.

Dave tried to guess from the coach's shouted code message what the play might be. He looked left, seeing that the wide receiver there was number eighty, a well-built Mexican-looking boy called Tony Croft. He'd been introduced to Dave and said he was a big fan of the San Francisco Forty-Niners' wide receiver, Jerry Rice, who also wore number eighty.

At the snap from the huddle, Tony ran about twenty yards down-field, planting his left foot and turning sharply inside, leaving the defender helplessly stranded. Chip, with all the time in the world, threw from the pocket, sending a perfectly-weighted pass, right on the numbers on the chest of the wide receiver.

Dave applauded the move. 'Simple, but effective,' he thought to himself.

'Soon be time to break for lunch,' said Haffkine. 'If you like, I'll take you and Chip and a couple of the other guys for a burger and a shake. How's that sound?'

'Fine, thanks.'

'You're welcome. But we'll have a bit of fun for you. You and the other two quarterbacks can try the pass-throwing test.'

'What's that?'

'Wait and see.' Raising his voice. 'One last play.

Gold-digger trap lock, Chip. Make it a good one. Get us ready for Oakland.'

The young quarterback adjusted the strap on his helmet, bending into the huddle of players. 'Gold-digger trap lock,' he shouted. 'We gotta have it. Go for it.'

He slapped hands with the centre, and took up his position. Again, Dave admired the older boy. He was poised and very much the leader of the team. Even here on the rough piece of practice turf, at the back of the big Aquarium, he was psyched up and eager to play. Dave guessed he'd be just the same at a crunch moment in a big game. Like the one they had up and coming.

'This'd be a play for fourth and long when we're in trouble. Chip's got to put the ball on a nickel from thirty yards. Imagine time's oozing away, Dave. Only other alternative would be a real high ball to drop in the end-zone with all your eligible receivers goin' up for it.'

Dave nodded at what Ray Haffkine was saying. 'They call that one a 'Hail Mary' pass, don't they?'

The coach looked down at him with increased respect. 'They surely do, Dave. Hey, you really know your gridiron, don't you? Don was right 'bout you. Mebbe you're not that big, yet, but you got the makings, son. Here we go.'

It was a simple play.

The team's speed man, receiver number eighty-nine, Ben Michaels, went for a flat burn, sprinting as hard as he could, long legs pumping away like pistons, while Ron yelled encouragement at him. He outran the panting corner-back and was three yards up as he broke into the end-zone. Chip Altman cocked his arm and threw an inch-perfect rainbow pass, the ball slicing though the warm morning air, eluding the clutching fingers of the desperate corner-back, landing clean in the arms of the receiver.

'Great play,' said Dave.

Mike Pomfret had joined them, standing with his helmet dangling from his right hand, morosely chewing gum. 'Coulda done better,' he mumbled.

'Sure you could,' said Ray Haffkine. 'It's not your arm or your eye, son. We both know that. It's a question of your temperament. That's why Chip is starter and you aren't. Work on it.'

'Yeah, yeah. Can we have a pass competition now? Can we, huh?'

'Sure. Like a try, Dave?'

'Please. I don't think . . .' he began, talking to Ray's retreating back. But Pomfret interrupted him in a stage whisper. 'Chicken little English retard.'

Dave decided that he would show the loudmouth and put him in his place.

It's a shame how life often doesn't work out quite like you hope.

Dave felt more nervous than he'd done for ages. Even waiting for the kick-off in the big final at the end of the last season hadn't been as bad as this. Ray had called all the other boys off the squad together, and they sat around watching. Alix Cassady stood with half a dozen other girls to one side of the field. She saw Dave looking in her direction and gave him a wave of encouragement.

'Simple game, Dave. Chip and Mike generally do it during their own training. Just a test of throwing accuracy. Tony Croft, our top receiver, is the target. He has to stand still and you have to try and hit him right on the numbers. No diving and jumping to take it. First pass is from ten yards. Then up five yards at a time to forty yards. That's the best we expect at this level of gridiron.'

'Let's go,' said Chip. 'Show us how good you English are.' But he said it with a friendly mockery.

'Mebbe we should start at one yard for the retard,' hissed Mike Pomfret. Trying to put Dave off.

To his dismay, Dave could feel that the loutish boy had succeeded. He felt tense, the muscles tight in his hand and arm and shoulder. It was some days since he'd last thrown a football, never thinking that he might get a chance to do it here in San Francisco. And the thought that they might give him the opportunity to actually come in for a play for their big match against their Oakland rivals made it even worse.

'Ten yards, Tony,' called Ray Haffkine. 'Chip. Show us all how to do it.'

Chip took the ball, almost casually, pitching it at the stockily built wide receiver, who stood perfectly still, taking the pass in the centre of his chest. Right on the numbers.

Mike Pomfret was next, swaggering to the mark, catching the return throw from Tony Croft. Spitting on the grass in Dave's direction. 'Watch the experts, mutant,' he called.

The pass was spot-on accurate, the ball spiralling on its long axis, clean into the waiting hands of the wide receiver.

'Your turn, Dave,' said Ray. 'Take your time, son. No hurry.'

'Sure,' muttered Pomfret. 'We got the whole day to wait.'

Dave swallowed, finding his mouth dry. But he was sweating with nerves, the palms of his hands slippery. He wiped them on his jeans, taking long, slow breaths to try and calm himself.

He gripped the ball, looking at the waiting receiver. When he played for the Downham Destroyers he'd pass three and four times this distance to Will and the other players, without a second thought. But this was different.

Dave took a final deep breath and launched the pass.

★★★★★★ The moment he let it go, Dave knew
4 it was a dreadful pass. The ball bob-
bled off his fingers, slipping sideways,
rolling clumsily end over end, hitting
★★★★★★ the turf a good ten feet to the left of
the waiting boy. In the sudden
silence, Dave heard a snigger run around the American boys, led by Mike Pomfret. 'What'd I say, guys?
The kid's a real grade one numb-brain.'

'Shut up, Mike,' snapped Ray Haffkine. 'Don't
worry, Dave. Have another shot.'

The second time was only fractionally better. By
leaping to his right Tony Croft just managed to scoop
up the ball, rolling on his shoulder and coming up
with the pass.

'You want another try, Dave?'

'No thanks. I'm . . . well, I'm not warmed up or
anything. I feel tight.'

'You look loose, retard,' sniggered Mike Pomfret.
'Mebbe if Tony moved about nine yards closer you
could sort of hand it to him.'

'I said to shut up, son,' warned the coach. 'All
right, guys. That's it for today. Training again day
after tomorrow.'

The boys began to drift away. Dave stood where he
was, bitterly disappointed at how badly he'd done.
The first one had been a real sloppy eggbeater of a

pass. And the second one was also terrible. What was so upsetting, bringing a prickling feeling to the back of his eyes, was that he knew he could do much better. Maybe not so good as Chip Altman, but good enough not to have made such a fool of himself. He felt utterly, thoroughly miserable about what he'd done.

Alix Cassady left the other cheer-leaders and walked across to him, joining Chip Altman and Tony Croft, who'd also stayed behind. Ray Haffkine was talking to a couple of the linebackers, glancing over his shoulder at the English boy.

'I can do better than that,' said Dave, desperate that the others believed him.

'Sure,' said the receiver.

'I've got a fifty-eight per cent completion rate back home on passes.'

'That's one per cent better than mine this season,' said Chip Altman. But his voice was oddly neutral, and Dave couldn't tell whether the San Francisco boy believed him or not.

'What's your record on interceptions?' asked Tony Croft.

'Only half a dozen all season.'

'I'm sorry?' said the boy, looking puzzled. Dave couldn't tell whether it was just the English accent or whether it was the expression 'half a dozen'.

He tried again. 'Six times.'

'That's real good,' said Alix. 'But how many times did they get to you? To sack you?'

It was the one statistic that Dave had never checked on. His coach, Tom Nickleby, would have known. 'I guess it's not more than one or two times per game.'

Chip laughed. 'That's a fine record. Guess you were just kind of nervous in front of everyone. I got sacked eight times a few weeks back. Palo Alto. Remember that one?' asking Alix and Tony.

'Sure,' said the girl. 'Our offensive linesmen had been partying the night before and they played like they were still asleep. Boy, you took some knocks that day, Chip, on account of those nerds.'

'Flappermouth Pomfret came on the final quarter,' said Tony.

'How did he do?' asked Dave.

Chip answered. 'Mike's a problem. His old man's a sponsor, so he can't be cut from the squad. And in practice he's real good. His arm's as strong as mine. Good passer. Put him in a game and he can't . . . I don't know. Seems his nerve's not good enough.'

'Or his heart,' said Ray Haffkine, rejoining the four teenagers. 'He'll learn. One day.'

'What happened when he came on against . . . what was the name?'

'Palo Alto,' replied Chip. 'Got sacked three times in four possessions. Started throwing too early. I had to come back in.' He shook his head ruefully at the sad memory. 'Only loss of the season.'

Ray Haffkine looked at Dave. 'Your uncle asked me to arrange some company for you today. Chip's mom's due right now. She'll take the two of you around. Show you some more of the city. And then drop you back at the apartment for dinner. That sound OK with you?'

'Sure, Ray,' said Dave, feeling better already, liking

46

the three others with him. Tony seemed a nice guy, and Chip was so professional. He liked Alix Cassady, too. She obviously knew a lot about the game.

'Can I come along, Chip?' asked Alix.

'Sure. How 'bout you, Tony?'

'Can't. Gotta split. Promised to wash the old man's car for him by two so's he can go play golf in it with his office buddies. They call it an out-of-office meeting.'

Everyone laughed. Ray shook Dave's hand. 'Good to meet you, son. You want to come to another session, you're real welcome. And I still mean what I said 'bout you mebbe coming in for a play.'

Dave was amazed. 'After I mucked up on that throwing? Really?'

'For sure, Dave. Show me a quarterback who says he never flunked a pass . . . and I'll show you a damned liar. See you Wednesday.'

He and Tony went off together, leaving Dave with Chip and Alix. The weather was still marvellous. A big air-balloon drifted lazily over the city behind them, advertising a festival of folk music across the Bay at Berkeley, on the campus of the University of California.

'If your mom doesn't show, we could go swimming,' suggested Alix. 'You got a towel and stuff, Dave?'

'Back at the flat . . . I mean, the apartment.'

'Hey, you ever been in a jacuzzi?' asked Chip. 'They got a new one at the pool downtown.'

'What's a . . . what you said?'

'Hot tub. Lots of jets of air and bubbles pump through it. You got to try it sometime.'

Dave wasn't sure he really liked the sound of it. But he was saved from committing himself to the idea by the arrival of Mrs Altman.

Afterwards, when he thought about it, Dave decided that meeting Debby Altman for the first time was a bit like being hit over the head with three hundredweight of noisy pink icing-sugar.

She was around forty, with frizzy blonde hair, showing suspiciously dark around the roots. Dave's guess was that she weighed in around twelve stone. She wore a pink and cream trouser suit with a huge *diamanté* brooch and dangling silver ear-rings shaped like snakes. Her feet were jammed into orange sandals with teetering heels.

Debby was also one of the kindest, nicest people that Dave had ever met.

She came wobbling towards him, arms thrown wide, a huge smile splitting her face in half. 'You must be Don, honey?'

He dodged neatly, but politely. 'No, that's my uncle. I'm Dave Sheppard.'

'Course you are, honey. Silly me. Welcome to San Francisco, dear. Your English accent is so neat.'

'Thank you.'

'You're welcome.' Suddenly aware that the two of them were not alone. 'Alix, sweetheart, lovely to see you. Chip, how did it go? You practise that running-back feint and cut left play I told you about? The one that Dan Fouts did for the Chargers in week four of last season?'

'Sure, Mom. Needs more work.'

'Get it right for the Oakland game, Chip.'

'Sure, Mom. We goin' to take Dave and Alix around the city some?'

'We surely are. If Betsy can manage us all. Alix, you best ride up front with me.'

Betsy was a black Volkswagen saloon, covered in stick-on silver stars. A lot of which were peeling off. Debby Altman drove like she talked. In impulsive, rapid bursts, sometimes taking both hands off the steering-wheel to point out something of interest.

Dave sat with Chip. Debby rattled on alternating between a guide of San Francisco and items of American Football interest. She was a walking encyclopaedia of the game, particularly on the history of the Forty-Niners.

'Dave plays quarterback in England, Mom,' said Chip. 'And he's a fan of the Forty-Niners.'

She squealed, turning round to grin at Dave, coming within a hair's breadth of wrecking a hot-dog cart and demolishing a demure line of black-habited nuns.

'Is that so, honey!? Then Joe Montana's your main man, is he?'

'Yes. He's sort of my hero,' replied Dave.

'My father and all three of my husbands have been Forty-Niners supporters. My father was a buddy of the great Joe Perry.'

'Guess you've never heard of him in England, have you, Dave?' asked Alix, turning round in the front seat .

'Sure. Number Seventy-Four. Used to play for the

49

Alameda Naval Air Station. He was the first ever player to have thousand yard seasons back to back. In, I think, fifty-three and four.'

The car was quiet, with even Debby Altman silent for once. She finally broke the stillness. 'Out of sight, honey! You surely know your football. Joe's still . . .'

'In the top ten rushers . . .' he finished. 'I know that.'

Chip punched him lightly on the arm. 'You're somethin' else, my man. How d'you know about old Joe Perry?'

'Uncle Don gave me a copy of an old book about the San Francisco Forty-Niners, from nineteen forty-five to seventy-two. In a series called . . .'

This time, everyone else in the car interrupted him, chorussing: '*Great Teams, Great Years*, Dave. We know.'

The rest of the day was all fun.

Dave found it hard at first to take the casual way Debby talked about her three previous marriages. She was currently between husbands. Chip didn't seem at all concerned either. In fact, Alix's father had been married once before and her current mother twice. And most of their friends seemed either to have single parents or be in the middle of some appallingly complex mish-mash of past and present marriages.

'And so I came in to find that *her* kids and *his* kids were both beating up *their* kids,' said Debby, laughing capaciously at the punchline of a joke that Dave had lost track of some minutes before.

He felt a bit embarrassed to have to admit that his parents were still married to each other after twenty-four years. Out here in California it seemed oddly like an admission of failure!

They went to the Maritime Museum, which was a great building of grey stone, shaped exactly like a large ship. From its windows they could see the Golden Gate Bridge, its arch already beginning to disappear beneath the daily mountains of fog.

Debby took the three kids to a shopping complex called Ghirardelli, with stores selling beautiful things in crystal and fabrics, and expensive jewellery. There she bought them some chocolates, raving about how wonderful they were. Dave was too polite to tell her that he thought ordinary English chocolates seemed just as good to him.

Chip told his mother that Ray Haffkine had promised Dave Sheppard a chance to go for a play against the Oakland Raiders youth team, if they were ahead. He didn't mention the awful showing that Dave had put up at the throwing test.

Dave really liked Chip Altman. And he also liked Alix Cassady. He found he could talk to her just as if she were one of the boys, without having to go into silly game-playing. Not that he minded playing games; just so long as he had some idea of what the rules were.

They ate lunch down on Fisherman's Wharf, not far from the Holiday Inn where Uncle Don worked. Alix had some fresh crab but Chip and Dave both ate the biggest pizzas he'd ever seen. Dripping with cheese, anchovies, tomato, peppers and olives. Dave could hardly hold his slice, but he managed to eat it all.

On the way back towards Uncle Don's apartment, Debby drove them down the most famous street in the whole of San Francisco, Lombard Street, which zig-zags like a broken backed snake, bending in on itself a total of seven times in only about a hundred yards. Traffic had to crawl down it, nose to tail, while tourists took photographs.

'Aren't the houses neat, Dave?' said Alix. 'I always figured I'd love to live here, in one of those houses. Look at the hydrangeas and lilacs on the walls.'

Dave didn't know what they were, but he admitted that the flowers were very pretty, though the winding little hill made him feel a bit sick, after the pizza.

There had been the double-scoop chocolate fudge ice-cream as well.

And the two cans of Coke.

Not to mention the bag of jelly beans.

And something that he thought was called a Mars bar, but turned out to have nuts in it and wasn't a bit like he thought it would be.

Debby dropped him off at the door. 'Want me to come up with you, honey?'

'No, thanks. And thanks a lot for the lunch and the drive and everything.'

'You're welcome, honey. You have a nice day now.'

'Bye, Chip. Bye, Alix. Thanks a lot. Been a great day.'

Chip gave him a wave of the hand. 'See you Wednesday, my man. If you want to get there early, I'll throw some with you. Before Mike the Mouth shows up.'

'Thanks.'

Alix also waved, leaning out of the front window of the bizarre little car. 'Nice to meet you, Dave. See you around.'

'Yes,' he said, standing in the quiet warmth of the late afternoon, watching as Debby drove off with a crashing of gears, smoke pouring from the exhaust. Dave thought it sounded as if the old VW was developing a defective silencer.

'No,' he said to himself, as the car swung out of sight. 'They don't call it a silencer. They call it a muffler.' He was pleased he'd remembered that.

Uncle Don was waiting for him when he came in, eager to hear all about how the day had gone. Dave told him everything. Trying to put the jumble of happenings into some sort of logical order.

That night his dreams were a strange mix of fat blonde ladies and men with ribbons in black beards and a cheer-leader with hair bleached white.

★★★★★★ It rained Tuesday.

Uncle Don was working again but Dave was quite content to have a relaxing day in the apartment. There were several of the NFL videos on a shelf and he promised himself one in the morning and one in the afternoon. Also, he decided that he'd send an airmail letter to his parents and one to Wilburn. The other thing he wanted to do was spend some time just flopped in front of the television, soaking up some American programmes. They were so different from English telly. He was specially fascinated by the commercials, relishing the feeling of being a stranger in a strange land.

There were two phone calls.

Around nine-thirty Chip Altman rang him. Just as he was spreading a thick layer of crunchy peanut butter on a slice of wholewheat bread.

'Hi, Dave. How y'doin?'

'Fine, thanks.'

'You're welcome. Mom was goin' to ask you if you wanted to come to Marine World today, but the weather's so lousy . . . It's a kind of big zoo and aquarium with shows and dolphins and killer whales and lions.'

'Sounds real thin.'

'What? Didn't catch that, Dave.'

54

'Doesn't matter, Chip. Thanks anyway for the offer. Maybe another day.'

'Sure. See you tomorrow?'

'You bet.'

'See yer, Dave. Bye.'

The next call was around eleven, when Dave was locked into the NFL video of 'Hits And Hitters', wincing at some of the crunching tackles. Admiring, as he always did, the great power and beauty of the gridiron game. Deciding that he *would* do better at the throwing tests with the Junior Forty-Niners, and not let that unpleasant Mike Pomfret put him off at all.

The phone made him jump.

Dave picked up the receiver, reading the number off the dial. Hearing the flat, West Coast accent of Alix Cassady.

'Hi. Great weather here in the city, huh?'

'Makes me homesick for England,' he replied, looking out of windows that were streaked with pattering rain.

'Just wanted to ask if you wanted to come with us on a mystery trip on Saturday?'

'Where to?'

She laughed. 'Dummy! It's a mystery trip. My dad's organised it for the team, as kind of a good luck for the big one next week. I guess we might go some place like Alcatraz. It's good fun there. You been?'

'No. I'd like to.'

'Sure thing, Dave. My dad's really interested in you bein' a fan of the Forty-Niners. He said that he could try . . .' She stopped and he heard someone in the background calling something to her. A man's voice. He guessed it was her father. She came back on the line again. 'Sorry, Dave. Dad says not to tell any more. In case. I'll tell you 'bout Saturday at training tomorrow. You will come, won't you?'

'Yes.'

'Me an' Chip figured you might . . . you know, have been emotionally disrupted by the hassle with Mike the Mouth. You're in an alien and insecure situation.'

'No,' he replied. 'I got over it. One of those things, isn't it?'

'Guess so. But if you have a problem, my mother's been into transactional analysis and she could recommend a good shrink for you.'

Dave wrinkled his forehead. It sounded like Alix was wondering if he needed a psychiatrist! Maybe he hadn't understood her properly.

'Thanks. If I need that, I'll ask you.'

'You're welcome. See you tomorrow, Dave. Have a nice day.'

'And you.'

Around two, he finished the letter to his parents. Because mail took about a week to get home, there was no point in writing later in the holiday. A week on Sunday and Uncle Don would be taking him to the airport to put him on a flight back to England, changing at New York.

'Missing you all. Uncle Don said to tell you that everything was fine. Might go to Alcatraz on Saturday with Chip and some of the other guys.' Somehow, he couldn't work out how to mention Alix Cassady, without risking some heavy-handed teasing from his father and brothers when he got home.

Dave signed the letter and put it in the flimsy airmail envelope, sticking it down carefully, remembering to put the address of the apartment on the back, like Uncle Don had told him.

He was feeling peckish, so he went and opened the door of the massive white refrigerator. There was a magnetic pink pig stuck to the side, holding a label that said: 'EAT+EAT=FAT'.

That didn't worry Dave.

He poured himself a glass of orange juice from the waxed container, finding some thin slices of smoked ham and some cheese with big holes in it on the top shelf. Making himself a sandwich on rye, squirting some ketchup on top to give the meal more of a touch of class.

Dave washed up and put the plate and knife neatly in their places, in a way that would have delighted, and surprised his mother, if she'd been there to see it.

He put a Springsteen album on the turntable, choosing the side with 'Darkness On The Edge Of Town' on it, and picked up his felt-tip to write to Wilburn.

The letter dealt mainly with food eaten and with American Football seen on video or discussed or watched with the Junior Forty-Niners. He told Will about Chip Altman, editing out any reference to Mike Pomfret. For some minutes he considered whether to mention how nice Alix Cassady had been, but in the end he left it out. Even with the best mate in the

57

world, there were some things that were better kept private.

As he laboriously filled the page with news, he thought about tomorrow and the training session with the youth team. If he did as badly as that in the throwing test again, common sense told him that there was no way that Ray Haffkine could put him in for the Oakland match.

No way at all.

After Uncle Don came home from work, they ate a takeaway Vietnamese meal together. Dave liked the pineapple and rice with prawns, but found some of the vegetables with shredded chicken a little too flavoured with spices for his taste.

Before going to bed, he talked to his uncle about the problems of tension that he'd felt with Mike Pomfret needling him and the other American kids staring at him.

'You've played in front of crowds before, Dave. What's different?'

'There I knew I could do well. This isn't the same. American Football's their game. Not mine. Not as a . . . I don't know . . . as a right, I suppose. I feel that I come over here and if I'm goin' to do it, then I've got to be better than any of them.'

Uncle Don stood up, bending to look at the row of videos. He picked out the one on quarterbacks, with a picture of Joe Montana on its cover.

'Here. Let's watch this before you go off to bed, young man. You worry about wantin' to be good. What can I tell you? I've seen you, and you're very

58

good. I'm not an NFL coach, but I reckon you've got true . . . I almost said true genius. Maybe you have, Dave. Go out there tomorrow and throw the football and show 'em. Show 'em all.'

Everyone whooped with delight, except Mike Pomfret, as Dave threw his fourth successive pass to Tony Croft. The wide receiver's broad, tanned face broke into a smile. Looking across to Ray Haffkine, who was also grinning at the success of the young English boy. 'How d'yer like them apples, Ray?' he yelled.

The coach raised finger and thumb, bringing them together in a circle, showing his approval. 'Fine, son,' he growled. 'Tony, move on back to the thirty.'

The boy paced off five more yards away, waiting for the three quarterbacks to take their throws. So far both Chip and Dave had thrown perfect completions each time. Mike had thrown one good pass, followed by a poor one, followed by two misses.

And he was getting rattled. After the fourth throw, with his ball wobbling yards to the right, Dave had said, *very* kindly, 'Jolly bad luck, Mike. Maybe if Tony moved about twenty-four yards closer, then you could pass it to him.'

Pomfret had sworn at him, getting an automatic one dollar training fine from Coach Haffkine.

Chip threw a good rainbow to Tony Croft, on the numbers. Mike Pomfret stepped up to take his throw, watched in silence by the rest of the squad.

'Come on,' yelled Alix Cassady. 'Show that English retard how it's done, Mike.'

'No, I've hurt my arm,' he snapped, dropping the

59

ball on the turf and stalking away, picking up his jacket as he went, leaving the field.

'Your ball, Dave,' said Ray.

Tony caught the thirty yard pass without having to move a step in any direction. Everyone applauded.

At thirty-five both boys reached the receiver, though Dave felt he was nearing his own limits. Chip's pass at forty yards was taken by Tony, but he had to side-step a couple of paces to make the catch.

'Go, Dave,' urged Chip.

Dave moved the ball in his hands, staring intently at it, psyching himself for one of the longest throws he'd tried. When he and Wilburn practised at the park round the corner from their homes, he'd sometimes guesstimated that he could throw a good forty-yarder. Now he had to do it.

He wiped his fingers down the thigh of his jeans. Opened index finger and thumb to grip the pointed end, middle finger touching the laces, to add spin. Cocking the arm back, looking at Tony Croft. The receiver seemed a very long way off from him.

'Go,' he whispered to himself.

Uncle Don poured himself a can of Budweiser beer from the fridge. 'And it was a good completion?'

'Yes. Tony never had to move an inch. It was a great pass, Uncle Don. Ray Haffkine said that he was getting in touch with the people in charge of the league to register me. Seems they can do that under special conditions.'

Dave could hardly believe it.

A week Saturday and he now believed there was a genuine chance he'd get on the field to play for a team in San Francisco. Beyond his wildest dreams.

And there was still so much holiday to come.

★★★★★★ At Ray Haffkine's suggestion, Dave spent part of his spare time with Chip Altman, learning some of the playbook of the Junior Forty-Niners.

★★★★★★ He wasn't surprised to find that it was more complex, with more advanced plays than the ones they used back home for the Destroyers. Generally speaking in England, Tom Nickleby kept in the same offense for first, second or third downs. Here, Ray had some variations, depending on what sort of passing or rushing play was going to be called.

'Just try and memorise about a dozen of the basic calls,' said Chip. 'Then, if you get on, Ray'll make sure that he sends in one of the plays that you've learned. It'll be great.'

Dave realised that Alix's father must be pretty wealthy. He'd hired a whole boat just for the Junior Forty-Niners and a few friends and family. Altogether there were about a hundred of them, filing on board the red and white boat, down at the end of Fisherman's Wharf in the bright sunlight of Saturday morning. The Golden Gate Bridge across the narrows at the neck of the Bay seemed almost to glow like spun gold. Behind them the city rose away in tiers, like an architect's wedding-cake, with the pyramid of the

TransAmerica building as its centrepiece. Helicopters, taking tourists on rubbernecking tours over the calm water, buzzed across the sky, landing and taking off at regular intervals.

Uncle Don was working that morning, but he'd agreed that Dave now knew his way around that immediate part of San Francisco well enough to be trusted out on his own for a few blocks. Providing he didn't go wandering off into places he didn't know.

Chip was already on the quay, a camera slung around his neck. There'd been a long discussion back in England about whether Dave should take his father's camera or not. In the end it was decided not. In the first week Dave'd been too busy to worry much about it. But this morning he regretted not having it. While they waited, he mentioned it to Chip.

'Listen, Dave, you just tell me what to shoot for you and I'll take it. Then I can send you the pix when you get back. Here, let's have a few of the guys now.'

By then most of the squad had arrived, and Chip organised them into a line-up, putting Dave at the centre. Mike Pomfret insisted on standing away on one side, a scowl hanging loosely on his spotty cheeks.

Ray Haffkine bustled up, organising everyone on the boat. Alix was with him, coming over to join Dave, Chip and Tony Croft.

'Hi, guys. Great day for the trip. It's to Alcatraz then back here for a Chinese lunch. How does that sound?'

'Terrific,' they replied, in chorus.

* * *

Dave asked Chip to take a picture of the Golden Gate Bridge, and of the city, glittering like a magic palace, receding behind the foaming wake of the boat. Containers of fresh buttered popcorn had appeared, and everyone was tucking in. Seagulls hovered, motionless, waiting for scraps from the boys.

The island grew nearer, long and flat, with the buildings becoming clearer. Dave knew that it had been one of the most famous prisons in the world and that the gangster, Al 'Scarface' Capone had been held there years ago, but he didn't know much more than that.

Alix filled him in on some of the details. 'One of the National Parks Rangers will take us round. You have to stick with the tour and don't wander off. Those guys are real strict.'

'Sure are,' warned Chip. 'Make sure you don't drop litter or step out of line. They run a tight ship out there. Well, a tight island, anyway.'

'The name comes from the Spanish,' said Alix. 'Isla de los Alcotraces. Means island of the penguins. You see some pelicans there, but no penguins. Not I ever heard of. Used to be a military barracks, then it was taken over as a maximum security federal prison. Closed in sixty-two by Bobby Kennedy, when he was Attorney-General.'

'Cost forty thousand dollars a year per prisoner by then,' added Tony Croft, leaning on the rail, staring intently down into the frothing waters.

'The Rangers'll lock you in the punishment cells,' said Chip, gleefully. 'Double doors like a cell within a cell. Pitch dark. Total silence. No furniture at all. Cold.'

'Not even a toilet,' said Alix, trembling with mock terror. 'No clothes even. That's what it was like back then.'

Mike Pomfret was walking by and he nudged Dave hard in the side. 'Sounds a good place to keep a retard like you and throw away the key.'

Dave had taken enough from the bullying American boy and he turned angrily, fists clenched.

'Listen, you fat thug, I'm fed up with you tryin' to needle me! You want to fight then I'm ready for you. If you're too chicken, then just keep away from me! You hear me?'

Pomfret, bigger than Dave by a couple of inches, took a couple of steps back. 'Hey, man, keep cool. Can't you English take a joke?'

'Yes. You're the biggest joke of all, Pomfret. You can't play. Got no bottle. I'm miles better than you and Chip's out of sight as a quarterback.' Stepping in close to the boy, poking him in the chest with a finger. 'Just keep away from me. All right?'

Dave didn't very often lose his temper, but right at that moment he almost hoped that the American boy would give him an excuse to start a fight. To work off the aggression he felt.

'All right, all right,' mumbled Mike Pomfret. 'Jeeez, you sure make a fuss 'bout nothin', don't you?'

Dave watched him slouch away towards the bow of the boat. Chip patted him on the arm. 'Great, Dave. He's had that comin' for years.'

'Sorry I lost my temper a bit,' said Dave. 'Shouldn't have let him get to me.'

'Sure, but don't worry,' said Alix. 'Just enjoy the trip.'

Like so many things that he saw around San Francisco, Dave was knocked out by the island of Alcatraz. The dock where they got off the boat was grey and dull, with ominous buildings towering over them. They split into groups of around thirty, each with a Ranger, in khaki uniform and a hat like a Canadian Mountie. Dave was with Alix, Chip and Tony, as well as Mike Pomfret. Their Ranger was a young lady with horn-rimmed glasses, who was a mine of fascinating information about the old prison, leading them up the hill, towards the main entrance.

They visited the dining-rooms and the rows of cells, one above the other, the doors all controlled by a single master lever.

'Food was excellent here on the rock,' said their guide. 'And there were several comforts, though some aspects of life were tough. Inmates had real hot showers, as often as they liked. The water in the Bay's very cold, with treacherous currents. The authorities figured that if prisoners were well-fed they'd not want to escape. And the showers were *only* hot, so they couldn't get used to what the cold water might be like.'

Dave asked her how many prisoners Alcatraz had held when it was full.

She smiled at him. 'Nice to have an English visitor here. Welcome to the rock, young man. The cellblocks held between two hundred and fifty and three hundred inmates. Cells were nine by five by seven. This one here was one of them done up specially for the Clint Eastwood movie, *Escape From Alcatraz*. Three periods of association, each day, twenty minutes each. Two hours Sunday. We'll go out in the yard later for you to see what it was like.'

'Thank you,' said Dave.

'You're welcome.'

'Which was Al Capone's cell?' asked Chip Altman.

'Over in Block B,' replied the Ranger. 'Number two hundred on the second level.'

They went outside into what had been the main exercise yard, blinking in the bright sunlight. Dave found it really odd, to be able to stand there and see the city of San Francisco, seeming only about a quarter mile off. So near and yet so impossibly far. The guide had told them there was no proven record of a successful escape, though she conceded that as many as five men might have got away over the years.

She led the way around the outside of the island, above steep cliffs, where Dave saw the pelicans that Alix had mentioned. Mike Pomfret picked up a stone and skimmed it at the birds, earning a swift and very stern telling-off from the Ranger.

'Isn't it beautiful, out here?' said Alix to Dave.

Apart from the closeness of the city, he was amazed at the beauty and colour of parts of the island. The inmates and the guards had planted flowers, and over the years since it closed they'd run wild, added to by seeds dropped by passing birds. Away from the derelict and fire-scorched buildings, there were banks of blazing magenta and yellow.

They finally returned to a sort of visitors' centre with pictures and books about the penitentiary. Glancing over his shoulder, Dave saw Mike Pomfret sidle into one of the quiet corners of the arched building. But Chip was calling his attention to some photographs on a display and he forgot about the reserve quarterback.

For a few minutes.

'Guess it's nearly time for us to head back to the boat,' said Ray Haffkine, trying to gather the squad together.

But he was interrupted by an angry shout from the Ranger. 'I want all you guys through here, right now!' she called.

The group followed her voice, finding themselves in a blind alcove. The woman, face flushed with anger, was pointing at the far, blank wall.

'This was not here fifteen minutes ago, and you are the only party through here. Who is responsible for it? Come on.'

Someone had taken a piece of soft chalk and written a single word there, in large letters.

ALIX.

'Oh, no,' breathed the girl, standing between Dave and Chip.

'Who did it? Will Alix please step forward, whoever she is?'

'It's me, ma'am, but I didn't . . .'

'Did your parents teach you nothing about the way to behave, young lady? Defacing a national park in this mindless and irresponsible way. Have you no thought for your own heritage?'

'I didn't do it!' The shock of the accusation had brought the girl to the edge of tears, her voice shaking with tension.

'I suppose someone else wrote your name? There's nobody else called Alix with the group?' No answer. 'No, I thought not. Well, young lady, you and I had better have a talk and find out where you live. Your parents will be hearing from the authority about it and about the bill for cleaning it.'

'She couldn't have done it.'

'Who said . . .? Ah, the young English boy. And how do you know?'

'I've been with her ever since we came in here.'

Which wasn't strictly true, but Dave had a very good idea who'd done it. And it wasn't the girl.

'Well . . .' her expression softened as she realised she might have been wrong. 'If that's . . .'

'Mebbe he did it. The English kid.'

Dave didn't have to look round to know whose voice that was. The nasal, accusatory whine of Mike Pomfret. Trying to get his own back.

'Did you, young man?'

'No, miss. Course not.'

'Then who did?'

The code against sneaking was barely too strong for Dave. He itched to tell how he'd seen Pomfret creeping secretly into the part of the building where the chalk marks had been found.

'I saw the English kid creep in here, ma'am,' said Pomfret, schooling his face into a mask of righteous disapproval. 'I've heard they have a lot of graffiti over in England.'

All eyes turned to Dave and he flushed. Realising he was caught. If he now told what he'd seen, it would sound lame and feeble. As if he was trying to push suspicion from himself. He looked again at the word 'Alix', seeing how thick and bold the chalk marks were.

And a desperate gamble came to him.

Pomfret hadn't finished. 'I've seen how he's soft on you, Alix Cassady. Must have been him.'

'Dave, you . . .' she began, turning to face him.

'Course not,' looking through the crowd at his accuser. The Ranger was right beside him, reaching in the pocket of her uniform for a notepad and pen.

'Best have your name, young man,' she said.

'If he's saying it was me,' he said, fighting for control over his voice, 'if he says that, then let him come and point me out right here. In front of everyone. Point his finger and then, if he does, I guess I'll have to admit it.'

Scenting triumph, the boy pushed through to the edge of the crowd, standing a step away from Dave, in front of the lady Ranger.

'It was him,' he snarled.

'Who, me?' invited Dave.

'You . . .' pointing at him with the probing index finger of his right hand.

It was a frozen tableau. The rest of the Junior Forty-Niners, watching, most of them looking embarrassed for Dave Sheppard. Ray Haffkine, shaking his head slowly in disbelief. Chip Altman, at

Dave's side, eyes narrow with anger at Pomfret's betrayal of his new friend. Alix, eyes still brimming with tears at having been wrongly accused.

The Ranger, staring at Mike Pomfret. Dave, also looking at the boy's pointing finger, feeling his own heart leap with delight.

It had worked.

'What's that on your hand, Mike?' he asked, casually. 'Looks to me like . . .'

The Ranger's hand came out like a striking rattler, gripping the American boy by the right wrist. 'Like chalk,' she concluded. 'It surely does.'

The white smear was unmistakable. Mike Pomfret stood still, mouth working nervously, as the Ranger held him in an iron grip. 'I didn't . . . It wasn't . . .' he stammered. 'Just a joke, that's all.'

Chip was exultant on the boat back to the city. 'How d'you like them apples, kid?' he kept saying. 'Sure sacked Mike the Mouth, Dave. Great. Ray Haffkine's goin' to call his pa when we land and tell him to come take his bad boy home. And I heard Ray tell him that he's going to drop him from the squad the very next time he steps out of line. Can't be soon enough.'

Alix was quiet, still shaken by the unpleasant scene. The Ranger had spoken both to her and to Dave, explaining that Mike's parents would be contacted over the damage to the wall. 'I'm real sorry about thinking it was you two guys,' she'd said. 'That was quick thinking to get the fat kid to point his finger. You saw him do it, didn't you?'

Dave had nodded. 'Sort of, miss.'

The woman had gripped him firmly by the hand. 'You did well, young man. Now have a nice day and forget this. Just remember Alcatraz as it should be.'

'Thanks,' said Dave.

'You're welcome.'

All of them, minus Pomfret, ate a great lunch at Shang Yuen's Chinese restaurant, down on the waterfront.

Where Dave had the first hint of the biggest and nicest surprise of his American holiday . . .

★★★★★★ Dave found himself sitting at a table in the corner of the large, pleasantly cool room, with Chip, Alix, Tony, Ben Michaels and the squat, heavily-muscled nose tackle, Zal Yerkowicz.

★★★★★★ They'd hardly sat down when a tall, distinguished man in a light grey suit and hair to match entered the restaurant. Dave nudged Alix and pointed to him.

'Looks like a refugee from "Dynasty", doesn't he?'

'Guess he does some.' She stood up and waved to the man. 'Hi, Daddy. Here we are.' As he joined them: 'Dave here's from England, Daddy. Thinks you look like someone out of "Dynasty", he said.'

'I'd have preferred him to say I looked like Don Johnson,' he replied.

Dave hoped for a moment that there would be a repeat of the famous San Francisco earthquake and he could sink out of sight. He was at least grateful for the deep shadows in the restaurant. Mr Cassady leaned over and shook him by the hand, nodding to the other boys round the table.

'Good to meet you guys. Hope everyone's hungry. Build up your strength for next week and the Oakland team. Zal, how 'bout a triple chicken and noodles? And a bowl of lettuce for you, Ben.'

The waiter came smiling over with the menus and

began to offer them around the table. Dave glanced at his and was amazed at the range of dishes, far bigger than he'd ever seen when he'd eaten Chinese back home in England. But Mr Cassady waved the menus away. 'Just bring us a selection, would you? One main dish each plus rice. You choose for us. And maybe an extra portion of chicken with lychees and abalone with those sugar peas.'

'No.'

Dave couldn't believe his ears.

Nor, it seemed, could Mr Cassady. 'I'm sorry?'

The Chinese waiter was inflexible. 'No. You order too much.'

'Only one dish each and a coupla spares.'

'That too much. One dish each enough.'

'We'll eat it all, won't we, guys?' appealing to the boys and his daughter. Who all nodded their agreement. Dave felt he could have eaten three portions on his own.

Finally, grudgingly, the waiter wrote it down, shaking his head and muttering what sounded like dire threats if there was any food left. Another waiter brought Cokes all round, including one for Mr Cassady.

While they waited for the food to arrive, Alix added to Dave's confusion and embarrassment by recounting the story of their morning on Alcatraz, including with some embroidery Mike Pomfret's attempt to cause trouble and how Dave had saved the day.

'Why, that little . . . Let me shake your hand, son, for getting young Alix here out of a deep hole. My thanks to you.'

74

Dave stood and sheepishly shook the man's hand, sitting down again. Sipping his drink and looking out through the windows as Alix and her father held a private, whispered conversation. Ending with the girl planting a huge, slapping kiss on her father's tanned cheek.

'Thanks, Daddy,' she said. 'Monday, then?'

'Sure, poppet, sure.'

Just then the waiter arrived, pushing a trolley that was loaded beyond the safety limit with the bowls and platters of food. Only then did Dave realise the warning had been serious. It seemed a vast amount for the seven of them to eat.

But they somehow managed it, helped by the monstrous appetite of Zal. 'We call him the human garbage disposal system,' grinned Chip.

During the meal, Mr Cassady – 'Call me Steve,' – addressed most of his conversation to Dave. Asking him how he liked San Francisco, quizzing him on his love and knowledge of American Football in general and the Forty-Niners in particular.

'Boy, you sure know the game, kid,' he said, wiping his mouth with a napkin and calling for ices all round.

As Mr Cassady was paying the bill ('check', thought Dave) Alix nudged him. He signed the American Express bill and then looked across to Dave. 'You busy Monday afternoon, son?'

'Training in the morning. Then I suppose that I'm free.'

'Fine. I'll call your uncle tomorrow and fix something up for the afternoon.'

'What?'

Steve Cassady tapped the side of his nose meaningfully. 'Wait and see, Dave.' He pulled back the cuff of his jacket, revealing the gold Rolex Oyster watch. 'Damn it! Look at the time. Got to run, guys.'

'Thanks a lot for the meal and the trip and all, Steve,' said Chip Altman, the others joining in with their thanks.

'That's nothing, guys. Just beat the heck out of those no-hopers from across the Bay.'

On Sunday, Uncle Don drove Dave out across the Golden Gate Bridge, peeling off left along a narrow, winding road to one of the local tourist attractions. He parked under the shade of some massive trees, getting out and stretching his legs. Dave was glad to have arrived as the bending road had brought on a touch of travel sickness.

'Here's Muir Woods,' said Don. 'After a week back at work it's nice to get a break here and some peace and quiet.'

Dave had noticed a curious thing. In the first couple of days in the city, Don's American accent had become rapidly stronger. Now the reverse was happening and he seemed to be becoming more and more English again.

A number of shadowed paths wound in amongst the groves of beautiful trees, sequoias and giant redwoods, towering skywards, in rich profusion. Uncle Don clearly loved the place, but, if he'd been truthful, Dave found it all a bit boring. Once he'd boggled at how big the trees were, there didn't seem much else to do. And there was a group of noisy German tourists, hogging all the best positions and taking endless photos while they barked commands at each other to stand here or there.

But there was a nice gift-shop, and he liked the sign that said: 'Do not molest trees and shrubs.'

On the drive home, as they were nearing the north end of the bridge, Uncle Don said, 'Man who built this wrote a poem about the redwoods. Joseph Strauss.'

'Yeah?' said Dave.

'"To be like these, straight, true and fine,
To make our world, like theirs, a shrine;
Sink down, oh traveller, on your knees,
God stands before you in these trees."'

'That's nice,' replied Dave. But most of his mind was roving ahead, wondering what the treat could be that was waiting for him tomorrow afternoon.

For nearly an hour at the training session in the Park, Monday morning, Coach Haffkine went through a dozen or so plays with Dave, making sure he understood them; drilling into him in what kind of situation he might be called on to come on and take them.

'Main thing is to show real speed in rolling out of the pocket. Oakland have a mean defensive end. Biggest boy in the league. Name's Tommy Axler. They call him the "Mean Machine". He's hard and fast and good. Chip can show you his scars some time. So you got to be fast.'

Dave didn't like the sound of Axler at all.

They went through some of the plays and Dave

77

didn't feel too bad. Didn't feel he let himself down in the practices. Afterwards Chip told him they all thought he'd done well. But he repeated Ray Haffkine's warning about the Oakland Mean Machine.

'Wears number Ninety-Nine.'

'That's Mark Gastineau's number,' said Dave, remembering that the New York Jets' player held the all-time NFL record for most quarterback sacks.

'Sure is. And Tommy's got a right to it. Any hesitation and he's in your face.'

'Dirty player?'

Chip shook his head. 'No. Very hard but very fair. No face-mask tugging or late roughing. Tommy'll be first up at the end of the game to shake your hand.

The horn on the Cassady's Cadillac sounded the opening notes of 'Rally Round The Flag', bringing Dave to the window of the Russian Hill apartment. He saw Alix waving up at him from the sidewalk. She was wearing a bright red Forty-Niners' playing shirt and white shorts. He waved back and ran to check his reflection in the long mirror just inside the bedroom door. He had on his clean jeans and NFL trainers. What to wear on top had taken a lot of thought. He had no idea where they were going but he'd guessed it wouldn't be anything too formal. In the end he'd picked his Dire Straits 'Brothers In Arms' tee-shirt.

Steve had the window down, leaning his head out into the sun. He grinned at Dave. 'Hi there, boy. Come join us in the front.'

The car was so wide that it looked like they could have fitted another three people on the front seat.

Dave sank into the soft maroon leather, and grinned at Alix, sitting in the middle.

'You ready for this?' she asked.

'Guess so.'

And off they went.

Mr Cassady played some bland Eagles' tapes on the quadrophonic system as they motored out of San Francisco. Dave could tell they were heading roughly east, towards the mountains. The highway carried signs to Sacramento.

But they looped around the outskirts of the city after about an hour and a half. Steve drove with his left arm hanging out of the window, humming to himself, occasionally asking Dave about life in England. He was specially interested in hotels and restaurants, but Dave couldn't give him much information.

Alix didn't talk much, but she would occasionally giggle and look at Dave.

They kept going along Interstate 80, north and east, towards Reno, Nevada.

'Shame you're not here in the season, Dave. Could have taken you out to Candlestick Park.'

'Oh, I'd have loved that, Steve.'

'Seen a match and tasted the atmosphere.'

'Maybe I can, one day,' he said, sadly.

'Sure. Watch old Big Sky Montana throwing the long passes and Jerry Rice pickin' them off for touchdowns.'

'I'd love to see Joe Montana play. Seen him so much on the telly and on the videos.'

For some reason, that started Alix off on another of

her silly giggling fits. For the first time since he'd met her, Dave began to think that she was maybe just like all the other girls back home.

They finally pulled off the highway, heading into a small town. Dave was distracted by Alix as they passed a sign and didn't see what it read. After a while they came through some gates, where Steve Cassady showed a couple of stern-faced doormen a pass. They bent and peered into the car, finally waving them all on through. Alix's father turned into a parking lot, already three-quarters full, and stopped. As the engine ceased purring, the air-conditioning also stopped and Dave felt the warm air outside flood into the car.

'You guys wait here a coupla minutes. Gotta see someone about something.'

Steve slammed the door with a solid clunk and strode off towards some buildings. Dave could make out some men in shorts and track suits running around and he thought he could also see some goal-posts. But the sun was reflecting from the windows of another building, bouncing spears of light into his eyes so that he couldn't be sure what he was seeing.

'Won't be long,' giggled Alix.

Right at the back of his mind, there stirred the faintest of glimmering hopes. But it was so far-fetched that Dave resolutely set it away from him. It wouldn't be that!

'Here comes Daddy,' squeaked Alix.

There were two people walking towards the car. One was Steve Cassady, in light blue cotton trousers and a tennis shirt.

'Who's the . . .?' began Dave.

'Ssh,' replied the girl. 'Just sit tight.'

'But . . .' he began again, Alix hushing him with a wave of her hand.

The cassette player was still on, with the Eagles singing something about living life in the fast lane. Alix leaned across and pressed the 'Off' button on the control console.

The two men drew nearer. The sunlight off the windows was dazzling, making Dave's eyes water to stare into it. Steve Cassady was laughing, throwing his head back, teeth flashing white. The other man seemed to be wearing red shorts and had on what looked like a motor-cycle crash helmet. He was very tall, towering over Mr Cassady, walking with the easy stride of an athlete.

'Get out the car, Dave,' hissed Alix.

He fumbled at the catch. By the time he'd figured how to open it, the two men were virtually on top of him. Now they blocked out the sun and he blinked up at their tall shadows.

'All right, Dave?' asked Steve Cassady.

'Sure, thanks.'

'You're welcome.' There was a brief pause, while Dave glanced up, trying to make out the features of the man under the crash helmet. Only, it wasn't a crash helmet.

It was . . .

'Joe,' said Mr Cassady. 'Meet Dave Sheppard from England. Dave, shake hands with Joe Montana.'

Monday, August 12th was a day that would be etched for ever in the memory of Dave Sheppard.

Through his contacts and work for the club, and having made sure to clear it first with the Head Coach, Bill Walsh, Steve Cassady was able to take the English boy for a couple of hours to the Forty-Niners' summer training camp. Dave was able to walk where he wanted and sit on the sun-baked grass, watching and listening. Trying to concentrate on every sight and sound, to store them up for ever in his memory.

That first electrifying handshake. The face under the unbuckled helmet, like the hundred pictures that Dave had at home. Narrow, friendly eyes, thin nose and the broad, open smile. Joe was wearing red shorts, with his number, sixteen, on the right thigh, the Forty-Niners' name and a football in white on the left thigh. He wore training shoes with white socks, just below the knees. A playing shirt, and a loose red track suit top over it.

Joe Montana said something to Dave as they shook hands. But however hard he strained his memory, he could never recall what the words were. His brain had slipped a gear and become momentarily paralysed. The first thing he knew was Steve Cassady speaking.

'Joe has to go train now, Dave. He's promised me a

signed photo for you and he'll try and find a couple of minutes later to maybe have a word about playing quarterback. I've told him that's your position.'

'Yes, it is. It is, isn't it? Yeah, that'd be . . . Oh, wow, that'd be great. I can't thank you enough, Mr Cassady. And you . . .' He didn't know what to call him.

'Name's Joe, Dave,' said his hero.

'I'm pleased to meet you. That sounds silly. I can't believe that I'm meetin' you, Joe.'

'Have a look around,' said the quarterback. 'Catch you later.'

'Yes. Bye.'

Joe Montana loped off, back to the training field at the rear of the buildings. Steve Cassady stood there, grinning with delight at the success of his surprise. Alix Cassady also got out of the Cadillac and stood by her father.

Dave shook his head, mouth dry, head spinning. Scarcely able to believe that it hadn't been a dream. He'd actually met Joe 'Big Sky' Montana, one of the greatest quarterbacks in the history of the National Football League. Shaken his hand. Was going to talk to him again later in the afternoon.

'That's just the fiercest knockout ever, Steve,' he managed to stammer.

'You liked it, huh? Just a small thanks from Alix and me for the way you stood by her on Alcatraz.'

His daughter grinned. 'Yeah. Thanks, Dave.'

For a moment he couldn't think of anything to say. Then he did. 'You're welcome,' he said.

★ ★ ★

During that most wonderful afternoon, Dave met Bill Walsh and even got to shake hands and collect the autographs of some of the top Forty-Niners. With Steve and Alix at his elbow, he wasn't in any danger of interrupting the training when he shouldn't, or getting in anyone's way.

The summer training camp is an absolutely vital part of any American Football team's year. Along come the young hopefuls to try out under the watchful eyes of the legion of specialist coaches. The kickers and receivers, the quarterbacks and the tight ends. The regular squad mingle with them, getting fit after the lay-off, all of them concerned to make sure they keep their places.

'How many of the previous year's team get cut at the end of training camp?' asked Dave.

Steve hissed through his teeth. 'Tricky to answer that. Mebbe a half dozen don't make it. But you got to realise, Dave, that it'll include some guys who might never even have gotten out on the field at all during the last season. Kind of fringe players.'

The fields around the training camp were dotted with groups of players, all engaged in what looked like different kinds of medieval torture.

Offensive linemen tried their blocking strength against padded metal frames. There was a sort of jungle gym of machinery packed with weights. There were Forty-Niners upside down and rights ways up, exercising every muscle known to man. To see some of the big players, like Russ Francis, stripped off to the waist working on his chest and stomach muscles was a truly awesome sight.

'I figure they generate enough power to keep San Francisco in electricity for a month,' joked Alix.

Steve explained that every single one of the regular team had exercises that were specially tailored just for him. Strength or speed or stamina was improved, depending on the player's position.

'Linebackers and the backs might each have a run target of around two to three miles per session. The real big guys might aim at one mile. See some of them in weight jackets. They sometimes train with around . . . three to four of your stones on.'

'What are the buildings?'

'Gyms for poor weather. Medical rooms. Physio and baths. Changing rooms. Lockers. R an' R.'

'What's that?'

'Rest and recreation. For the times that they aren't dying out there for the team. Or to get on the team.' Steve pointed to the far side of the field. 'They're all rookies. The young college guys who hope to catch the eyes of the coaches and get their chance to break into the big time.'

'How much can a top player earn, Steve?' asked Dave.

'There's basic salary. Plus win bonuses and point bonuses. Extra payments from the owners of the clubs if they're doing really well.'

Alix interrupted her father. 'But the big bread's in the peripherals, isn't it?' Seeing the look of bewilderment on Dave's face. 'Means for sponsorship deals and advertising deals and all that kind of thing. Merchandising if you get your face on watches or food or tee-shirts.'

Steve nodded at what his daughter had said. 'That's right, honey. For some of the guys, you can say that a million dollars a year is a baseline figure for them. And a little more for some.'

Dave saw that most of the coaches carried stop-watches. In some cases a row of them, set on top of a clipboard, and they were timing players in various exercises.

By the time he was there, the original hundred or more hopefuls had been pared right down, and Bill Walsh was probably within only a dozen or so of making his final selection of the starting squad for the season. The forty-five man roster.

One of the linebackers – Dave didn't recognise him from the side of the field – was undergoing a punishing spell of training. A defense coach was making him do sprints of fifty yards or so, backwards, changing direction in zig-zags at a shouted order. It made the English boy feel dizzy just watching him.

A group of offensive players were sitting in a huddled circle round one of the coaches while he read to them from a crimson folder. Dave wanted to go closer but Steve Cassady shook his head. 'That's the team's Playbook, son. Could be around three hundred different plays in there. Easier to get at America's gold reserves in Fort Knox than it is to get hold of that.'

'Three hundred!' Dave was astounded. 'We have about twenty-five back home and we sort of improvise around them.'

Alix smiled. 'I guess that's just one of the

differences between the Downham Destroyers and the San Francisco Forty-Niners, isn't it?'

'One day you ought to come across and see us play. I mean, we aren't sort of very good, you know, but it could be part of a holiday.'

Steve Cassady frowned. 'Black mark for you there, Dave. Little Alix has been buggin' me to take her to England for a coupla years but I figure she's not old enough to appreciate Shakespeare and Westminister Abbey and the White Tower of London and all that history and culture.'

'I am so, Daddy,' she protested.

'Well, we'll see . . .' he said, in that weak refusal that parents try when they know they're on a losing wicket.

It was close to five o'clock when Dave's heart bounced again in his chest. Joe Montana had left some wind sprints that he'd been doing and was walking towards him. With him was the looming giant figure of Fred Quillan, Number Fifty-Six, the six feet five inch, twenty stone centre, accompanied by the slighter reserve running back, Tony Cherry.

Joe was holding a football, still wearing his helmet, the strap dangling under his chin. All three men were sweating, but they all gave Dave a smile as Joe Montana introduced him to them.

'Coach Walsh says we got just five minutes to make you the best young quarterback in all England,' said Joe, grinning. 'So, what's your biggest problem?'

'I'm training with the Junior Forty-Niners,' said Dave.

'Great team,' agreed Fred Quillan.

'Coach Haffkine says he'll put me on as a sort of guest player if they're winning. Maybe for one play.'

'Then it better be good, Dave,' said Cherry.

'Startin' quarterback's Chip Altman. Big match's against Oakland. He says they've got a real tough defensive end they call the Mean Machine. Wears ninety-nine.'

Joe Montana shuddered theatrically. 'Gastineau's number. Seen him up close a few times.'

'So, to beat this Tommy Axler, Coach says I have to work at rolling out fast. And . . . well, I think you're the best at that, Joe.'

Montana nodded at the compliment. 'It's important, all right. Hey, Carl. Give us a minute. Want to show this English boy, Dave Sheppard here, about rolling out.'

Carl Monroe, Number Thirty-Two in the team, came over, in shorts and a playing shirt, like the others, his helmet hanging from his right hand. Dave knew that Carl doubled as a wide receiver and running back for the Forty-Niners.

'Sure. You want a timed pattern or what?'

'Just go around thirty and I'll hit you,' said the quarterback. 'Now, Dave, watch and learn.'

The four men went into a quick huddle. Looking on from the sideline, Dave was immediately impressed with the way they went about it. This might just be a brief lesson for a kid, but they took it in a deadly serious and professional manner. Joe crouched behind Quillan, who held the ball as if he was going to snap it. Joe Montana didn't call out any play, just shouting the count.

'Ready? . . . Hut, hut, hut,' the ball in his hands at the third yell.

It was magic. Poetry in motion.

Joe moved with an incredible fluidity, wheeling round and making a great fake to the charging figure of Tony Cherry. The feint was so good that Dave's eyes followed the running back, then went back to Montana as he realised how he'd been fooled.

Joe scrambled away in a wide arc, deliberately not looking for any pass receiver downfield. He rolled to the right, then suddenly stopped dead, planted his foot and threw in one easy, graceful movement, the ball spiralling in a perfect arc, to the waiting figure of Carl Monroe, around thirty yards away, who caught it and pretended to run it in for a touchdown, spiking the ball into the watered turf.

Dave applauded, clapping furiously. Over the far side of the field he could make out the white-haired figure of the respected coach, Bill Walsh. And he guessed that the magical afternoon was nearly at its end.

The four players came over to him. Joe took the football off Carl and tossed it to the boy. 'Right, Dave. One time 'fore we go inside. Do what I did. Speed away, don't show where you're going to pass. Feint to a running back. Then plant that foot to give you a solid base for the pass. Eyes on your target. And let her go.'

'Me? Me do it?' squeaked Dave, voice cracking in his surprise.

'Sure. One go. Make it good.'

'Want me closer?' asked Carl Monroe.

'No,' said Dave. 'If I can get it right, I can reach you.'

'Sure?'

'Yes,' he replied. Though his heart was fluttering in his chest as if it wanted to break out.

'Good boy,' said Joe Montana, slapping him on the back. 'You got confidence. That's a big chunk of the battle for a quarterback. If you don't believe you can do it, then you never can.'

Dave took the warm football, walking out to the centre of the field. Quillan reached for it, grinning broadly at him. 'Know the count?'

'On three,' he said.

'Right.'

Crouching behind the giant Forty-Niner, Dave felt like he was hiding at the back of a huge crimson wall.

'Ready,' he said. 'Hut, hut, hut,' barking out the timing calls.

On the third call Quillan snapped the ball back into his waiting hands. Dave tried to recreate in his mind the mental film of the way that Joe Montana had done it. He could hear Tony Cherry thundering up behind him and he feinted the pass to the running back, who whispered, 'Nice fake, kid,' as he cut away left.

The English teenager whirled around and ran to his right, making sure he didn't give away his intended receiver by staring at him too soon. Though with his excellent peripheral vision, Dave could see Carl Monroe running a pattern about twenty yards downfield.

Inside his head he heard Joe Montana saying: 'Plant that foot.'

He stopped, digging in, giving himself that firm, solid base for the thrown ball. Looking and seeing Carl glance back over his shoulder, waiting for the pass. Dave cocked his arm and let it go, knowing with a fierce exultation that it was good.

That it was better than good.

The ball spun away, hanging, perfection against the clear blue sky. Rolling on and on, smacking into the hands of Carl Monroe, who repeated his run-in and spike inside the end-zone.

Dave heard cheering from the sideline behind him and he turned round, punching the air exultantly at his own success. He saw that Steve Cassady and Alix were both applauding him. Joe Montana came walking over to him, holding out a hand.

'That was good, Dave. I mean it. You picked that up like a real natural.'

There couldn't have been any bigger or better praise for Dave.

The other members of the senior Forty-Niners squad all gathered round him, adding their congratulations. What was so terrific was that inside he knew they were right. It *had* been good, feeling like he'd been rolling out that way all his playing career.

'Now go and beat the pants off the Oakland boys,' said Fred Quillan, shaking Dave's hand. It felt like his fingers had been swallowed into a gigantic vice. But the big man was gentle with his grip.

Steve Cassady patted Dave on the back. 'Real good,

son. Now, these guys gotta go work or the coach'll be after my butt.'

Dave thanked everyone, getting a chorus of 'You're welcome' from the players.

A final shake of the hand from Joe Montana and he was left alone in the long-shadowed afternoon field, with only Alix and her father for company.

Uncle Don insisted on hearing all about the magical visit that evening. Not once, but twice. Every detail of who was there and who said what and who did what.

It was close to midnight before they finally went to their beds. Dave lay awake, watching the stars through a gap in the blinds, feeling happier than he ever had in his life.

During the remainder of his second week in San Francisco, Dave spent more time with the Junior Forty-Niners at their training sessions in the Golden Gate Park. When the word got around that he'd been out to the training camp and actually had a private coaching session from Joe Montana, his reputation with the rest of the squad went rocketing. The story was told and retold, often by Alix, until it seemed as though Dave had been out there taking Joe's place in some of the plays and Bill Walsh had wanted him to make sure he came back to San Francisco when he was a few years older.

Mike Pomfret had, predictably, behaved with his usual friendly charm. 'Guess an English retard needs all the help he can get.'

Ray Haffkine took Dave on one side at the extra training session on Thursday, leading him away from the rest of the players.

'Listen, son, I have to talk.'

'Sure.'

'I've heard all about your visit out to Rocklin to the Forty-Niners' camp.'

'Lot of it's been exaggerated.'

'I know,' sensing the English boy was embarrassed by it. 'Young Alix is the worst at turning a dime into

93

a dollar. But I also heard from Steve that you did good out there.'

'Really?' The Californian sun had already tanned Dave's cheeks, so the blush didn't show too much.

'Yeah. But what I want to say is that you have to remember just precisely what I said.'

'About me getting a play?'

The coach nodded. 'Right. If the game situation means it's safe to do so, then I'll put you on for one play. That's all I can do.'

'I know that. If the match is dead close then I wouldn't expect to go on.'

'That's good, Dave. Chip is starting quarterback and if all goes well I'll leave him on for the afternoon. Mike, for all his faults, is reserve quarterback and if anything happens to Chip, which the Lord forbid, then he goes on.'

'What if he got injured?' asked Dave.

Ray Haffkine grinned. 'Then you'll get the biggest chance of your entire football career.'

Uncle Don had asked for a couple of days off during the week, and the Holiday Inn had agreed. But the news of the Oakland game had changed all that.

'I was goin' to work on Saturday then have Sunday off to get you on the plane home,' he said. 'Not now. I need Saturday to watch the big game. So I'll have to go back to my boss and ask for that off and work during the week to make up for it.'

The rest of the week simply raced on by.

Dave found there wasn't time to go and do much more sightseeing.

94

Chip's mother took the two boys down to Marriott's Great America fun-fair, an hour's drive south of San Francisco at Santa Clara, where Dave experienced the thrills of the white-knuckle rollercoaster rides for the first time. Debby Altman rode everything along with him and Chip, whooping and screaming her delight and fear as the cars rolled and pitched on the tight curves. They all ate vast quantities of popcorn, burgers, ice-creams and soft drinks, which nearly came back again for Dave when he took a second trip on the Tidal Wave, with its eighty foot forwards and backwards loop.

One morning Dave got up very early and he and Uncle Don walked through the waking city, relishing the quiet and the clean, sea air. As they strolled past a small park on the edge of Chinatown, they saw a group of a half dozen very elderly Oriental men, doing their exercises. Sort of slow-motion kung fu, done with great poise and solemnity.

Friday afternoon, Don took Dave south of the city again, to Marine-World Africa USA, a big theme park that held performing dolphins and killer whales, alongside a complex where there were wild animal shows. It was a staggeringly hot afternoon, with the temperature up in the nineties. Dave was quite relieved when it was time to get back in the air-conditioned car and drive towards San Francisco, watching as the banks of fog came rolling in over the hills to the west.

Overlaying it all, like a counterpoint to the wonders of his American holiday, was Dave's awareness that the big match was growing closer all the time. It had been five days off.

Then four days away.

Only three days to go.

Day after tomorrow.

Friday night he went to bed early, watching the portable telly showing re-runs of the old BBC serial about Roman times, 'I Claudius'.

'Eat a decent breakfast,' urged Don.

'Don't feel very hungry. Feel a bit nervous, actually,' said Dave.

'Be a surprise if you didn't. Have another couple of rashers of ham and some more orange juice.'

The game was to kick off at two o'clock in the afternoon, over the Oakland Bay Bridge, in a stadium on the Raiders' home turf. All the team were to make their own way there.

Uncle Don went into work for the morning and Dave hung around the apartment. Both Ray Haffkine and Chip Altman had called him up by eleven, checking he was all right and had transport over the Bay. Uncle Don came home a little after noon.

'You're sure that the gear you've borrowed all fits?' he asked.

'Yes. Boots feel fine. My playing shirt'll carry the number ten. I do hope I can get on just once. Be something to tell the mates back home. Be really great if I could.'

They left the apartment at twelve-fifteen. Uncle Don had put on his San Francisco Forty-Niners sweater and was wearing his supporters' cap as well. They got in the car and Uncle Don pressed the starter. After a heart-stopping hesitation, the engine fired and

96

they were off. The bridge came sweeping up ahead of them, carrying them over the sparkling water of the Bay, towards Oakland. The sun was shining brightly and there wasn't a cloud in the sky.

Like nearly the whole of Dave's holiday, it looked like it was going to be a nice day.

It was a dreadful shock to see how many people there were in the stadium. The biggest crowd that Dave had ever played in front of was in the last final for the Destroyers. Here there must have been close on fifteen thousand crammed in the seats, most wearing the favours of the Oakland team. Since they were the away team, the Junior Forty-Niners wore white shirts with red numbers. The Raiders wore their familiar strip of black and silver.

Both teams were out on the pitch, testing the surface, at the same time. A few waved or called to each other, but there was no hostility or unpleasantness.

'Which one is . . . Oh . . . him!' gasped Dave, recognising the Oakland boy who must be Tommy Axler, the notorious 'Mean Machine'. The top age for the teams was about fifteen, but he looked a man, full grown. He stood well over six feet tall and must have weighed in around twenty stone. His black face broke into a broad grin as he spotted Chip Altman. He came over to them.

'You mine, Number Sixteen. Hear me, Chip? You are mine today.'

The two boys shook hands and Chip introduced Dave Sheppard to Tommy, telling him that Dave was hoping to come on for a play late in the game. Having seen the Mean Machine up close, Dave was suddenly not quite so sure.

'Well, good luck to you, my man. You get the ball, then you better roll out fast, or I'll be on you like a rash. Good luck.' He shook his hand and went to rejoin the rest of the Oakland boys.

Mike Pomfret had seen the confrontation and had gone very pale and quiet. 'You all right?' asked Chip.

'Mind your own business, Altman,' snapped the other boy. 'Just ate somethin' that don't agree. I'm goin' to call Ralph.'

Dave watched him go, puzzled. 'Who's Ralph?'

Chip grinned. He put his finger down his throat and mimed being sick. 'That's crying Raaaaaaaaalph,' he said.

The San Francisco team kicked off into a light breeze. On the sideline behind their bench, Alix Cassady led the cheer-leaders in one of their complicated routines, getting their own supporters shouting and applauding. Much to Dave's amazement there were cameras there from one of the local TV stations, covering the game.

On their first possession of the quarter, the Oakland team failed to move the ball ten yards forwards in their opening three downs and elected to punt on the fourth down.

The offensive linemen didn't do their job that well and Jimmy Taylor, the tall reserve running back, got past a feeble block and managed to get to the kicker, actually charging the ball down with his chest. San Francisco recovered the football at the Oakland nineteen yard line. After a running play, Chip threw a perfectly weighted twelve yard pass to the Number Eighty, Tony Croft, who clung on for the first score of the game.

Ray Haffkine leaped off the bench, arms high, cheering the touchdown.

Dave noticed that the Mean Machine very nearly got to Chip as he threw the pass and hit him a split second later. Not at all dirty, but Chip was off balance and went down hard, getting up slowly, limping a little as he came back to the bench.

'You all right, Chip?' asked the Coach, worriedly.

'Yeah. Just twisted my ankle some as I went down.'

The extra point was good and the Junior Forty-Niners led by seven points to nothing. They held that lead until the last two minutes of the quarter.

Ray Haffkine had warned his squad that the Oakland special team was about the best in California. They proved it on a Forty-Niners punt. Their kick returner, with great block support, ran the ball a full eighty yards for a touchdown. The extra point was good, bringing the score level at seven all.

Just before the first quarter ended, Tommy Axler managed to get up on the blindside to sack Chip Altman. The quarterback held on to the ball, but he was limping more as he came off the field.

The second quarter of the game was tough action all the way, with the defenses dominating. Chip managed to keep out of trouble, showing what a complete player he was, holding the team together under desperate pressure from the Oakland Raiders.

Half-way through the quarter, San Francisco had worked their way up to the Oakland thirty-two yard line. Coach Haffkine sent in two running plays in succession. On the first of them the Mean Machine broke completely through and delivered a crushing hit on the back with the ball. The second time, the Oakland middle linebacker covered across fast and took the ball carrier out of bounds. Which left Chip facing a third and eighteen situation on the Oakland forty.

Once more the American boy showed his talent, coming up with the big play when the odds were loaded against him. He floated a short pass over the middle, caught by the tight end, Mal Netzen, who ran it hard and fast, before a desperate tackle brought him down just five yards short of the end zone and a touchdown.

Dave was standing with the rest of the Forty-Niners, lining the edge of the pitch. Ray Haffkine beckoned to the heavily-built running back, Rik Seeburg, the team's specialist on short yardage.

The ball was snapped back to Chip, who slipped it to the charging Seeburg, who just managed to make the touchdown. Once again, the extra point was good. There was no further scoring in the second quarter and at half-time Ray Haffkine was happy to lead his squad off to their changing-rooms, leading by fourteen points to seven.

In the locker-room, the Coach didn't have too much comment or advice. He praised them for playing hard and well, remembering all their plays and all their tactics. Chip had an ice-pack put on his ankle, which looked sore and swollen. But he insisted that he'd carry on.

Dave did what he could to make himself useful, bringing soft drinks to anyone who wanted one, and helping with a few of the players who'd got strapping coming loose off their hands and wrists.

'Just keep doin' what you're doin' already,' said Haffkine to the squad as he prepared to lead them out for the second half of the game. 'Got them on the run. Just keep it up and no mistakes.'

Zal Yerkowicz, the nose tackle, had a streak of blood across his shirt, which he kept pointing out wasn't his blood. He clapped his hands together. 'We're goin' out there and we're going to be like a pack of wild dogs and we are going to have us some *fun*!' he shouted.

Oakland kicked off, the ball bobbling and bouncing deep into the San Francisco half of the field, eventually ending on the twenty-nine yard line. Ray Haffkine, consulting his play-book, sent the signals to Chip Altman for a pass play, which was successfully completed. Followed by another, with the pass reaching Tony Croft, the wide receiver. The two plays carrying the Forty-Niners just inside the Oakland half of the field.

Behind him, Dave could hear Alix and the other girls working on the insistent rhythm of one of their chants, urging the Forty-Niners to 'Go, go, go!!'.

Chip came over to the sideline, finding it difficult to hear anything because of the noise of the crowd. Ray leaned close, shouting in his ear. Doing what Dave had expected. Another pass play.

Unfortunately, it was also what the coach of the Oakland Raiders was expecting.

It was a seven man pass rush, putting on intense pressure with the outside linebacker chasing Chip out of the pocket. Downfield, Chip saw his halfback come open for a pass. Dave saw it happen, almost as if it were in slow-motion; Chip cocking his arm, ready to unload the ball, Tommy Axler sweeping around his block like a man swatting away a fly, hitting Chip moments before he released the football.

The quarterback went flying in the air, feet well off the pitch, knocked sideways by the immense force of the Mean Machine's tackle.

'The ball's loose!' yelled someone directly behind Dave in the crowd.

The Oakland nose tackle scooped the bobbling ball off the turf, running it in over fifty yards unopposed for the touchdown. While the kicker was getting ready, Dave watched Ray Haffkine, face furrowed with worry, carrying Chip Altman off the pitch, cradled in his arms.

'My ankle, Coach. It went worse that time. Oh, boy, that hurts.'

'Can you stand?'

Chip tried, leaning heavily on Haffkine on one side, Dave on the other. The English boy felt him testing his weight, giving a gasp of pain, the ankle crumpling under him.

'I can have ice on it . . .' said Chip, voice almost

drowned by the cheer of the crowd as the extra point was made. Fourteen points all.

Ray Haffkine glanced across at where Mike Pomfret was standing, helmet in his hand, face white as driven snow. 'Come on, you guys,' called the coach. 'You're on, son. Go and do it.'

'Mebbe Chip'll be all right in a while,' he stammered.

'Get ready, Michael. You're goin' on.'

Dave knew that the play that Ray sent in with the nervous boy was a simple dump-off to the halfback. Just to give Mike a bit of confidence at the start.

Watching carefully, he saw that Axler said something to Mike Pomfret as he walked by him. The reserve quarterback hesitated and looked back to the bench.

'That son of . . . He's tryin' to psych him out,' said Ray.

The ball was snapped back to Pomfret. Dave recalled from his own training that this play called for a timing pattern, with the ball held by the quarterback until the receiver was in position and ready. With the threat of Tommy Axler coming at him, Mike lost his nerve and threw a wild, wobbling egg-beater of a pass, far too early. The halfback was still running, his back to the ball, giving it on a plate to the Oakland corner back. He intercepted it cleanly and began to run hard along the sideline.

'Hit him, someone!' screamed Haffkine. 'Pomfret! You can get him! Go for . . .' His voice faded away as he saw, like everyone saw, the reserve quarterback deliberately slow down and fake a despairing dive at the heels of the Oakland player. Missing him by yards.

The kick for the extra point was good.

Twenty-one points to fourteen.

With disaster written all over the big electronic scoreboard, Dave Sheppard guessed that he wasn't likely to get on now for his one play.

While he waited with the rest of the team to get back on with the offense, Mike Pomfret brushed aside any comments or advice from the coach.

'He read the code wrong. Had his back turned. What a dumbo! And I slipped or mebbe I was clipped by someone. Or I'd have had that kid easy.'

When San Francisco regained possession of the football, Ray Haffkine again sent in a safe, short pass play.

They could hear Mike's ringing tones calling in the huddle for a totally different play.

'No,' gasped Haffkine. 'That's a deep ball. Chip can do it. Mebbe you could, Dave. Pomfret couldn't throw that far if he tried all year.'

He was right.

Tony Croft, wearing eighty, was the intended receiver. Mike took the ball cleanly, dropping back far too slowly. He threw around twenty yards, way short of the forty mark that the play called for. An Oakland Raiders linebacker, covering on the play, picked it off and ran it back to the Forty-Niners' thirty-five yard line.

Ray sent on the defense, who did brilliantly to hold the Oakland team on three downs, forcing them to go for a field goal. The kick was successful and the score moved to twenty-four points to fourteen.

On the Forty-Niners bench, there was only gloom and despondency. The cheer-leaders had gone quiet, and the sections of the crowd that wore the scarlet and gold favours of San Francisco were sitting in their seats, long-faced and silent.

Ray Haffkine called his squad around him, trying to lift their spirits. 'Come on, guys. Two touchdowns. That's all it takes.'

Mike Pomfret sat, swigging lemon squash, helmet kicked yards away from his feet. 'I've had enough. That Mean Machine plays dirty. I don't wanna get crippled like Chip.'

Ray Haffkine took three steps to stand in front of him. 'What the heck are you sayin', son? Tommy Axler plays hard and fast, but he's as fair as any boy in this league.'

'That's right,' added Chip. 'Come on, Mike. You can't just give up. It's . . . it's unAmerican.'

'Forget it,' snapped Pomfret. Then, to everyone's surprise he put his head in his hands and started to cry. 'Don't wanna play, I don't wanna!!!'

Ray turned to Dave Sheppard, standing at his side. 'You don't get on for one play, Dave.'

'Oh, all right, Coach,' trying to hide his disappointment.

'No,' said Ray Haffkine. 'You get on for the rest of the match. There's eleven minutes and nine seconds left in this third quarter. Go and do your best.'

Dave stared at the tall, bearded American, unable to believe his ears. He had to be joking.

Had to be.

★★★★★★ 'Let's hear a big round of friendly Oakland applause for the reserve quarterback for the Junior Forty-Niners. Number Ten, all the way ★★★★★★ from England, David Sheppard!'

There was generous clapping and Alix led her team of cheer-leaders into a leaping, kicking routine to try and rouse their supporters.

Chip hobbled over to Dave, who was trying to buckle up his helmet, finding that his fingers had all turned to thumbs. 'Good luck, mate,' he said, in a mock Cockney accent. 'Relax and play your own game. Don't let Tommy get to you out there.'

'Easy for you to say. You're safe and warm on the bench,' joked Dave, fighting to control the tremble in his voice.

'Use ice red left,' said Ray Haffkine. 'You know what that is?'

There was a moment of utter blankness, then it came back to Dave what the play was. Short pass to Tony Croft who'd be cutting across to the left.

'Sure.'

Just before he went to run on the field with the offensive unit, Dave was surprised when the Oakland coach, a middle-aged man with silver-grey hair, jogged across to shake his hand and wish him luck.

Dave went into the huddle, the rest of the Forty-

Niners team about him, all looking to him for the call. At that moment, he sensed the sour flavour of defeat. Chip was off for good and Pomfret had let them all down by completely losing his bottle. And here was the young English kid. It was going to be downhill for the rest of the match.

'What's the play?' asked Tony, staring at him anxiously.

Panic was still sitting leering on Dave's shoulder and he fought against the dreadful blankness. 'Ice red left,' he said. 'Let's go.'

He wished his knees weren't wobbling so much.

'Hut, hut, hut,' he called, trying to concentrate. But on the second syllable his eye was caught by the imposing figure of Tommy Axler. Catching his glance, the Mean Machine gave him a wide grin and a wink. In all his games in England, Dave had never actually felt intimidated, but he did at that moment. The tall black kid was so confident in his own ability.

The ball came back and Dave very nearly fumbled it. All he wanted to do in those split seconds was get the football away from his hands. He didn't even realise that Tony Croft was covered by the defense, down to the bone. To the right Ben Michaels was free, hollering for the pass, but Dave threw it out towards Tony. The covering Oakland free safety picked it off like taking a ripe peach off the tree and began to run it back. Dave heard the moan of dismay from the crowd as they saw another touchdown on the way.

'No,' hissed Dave to himself, through gritted teeth. He might have fouled up on the play, but he wasn't going to throw it away like Pomfret had. He dodged a block and dived in at the sprinting Oakland safety, hitting him perfectly, knocking him crashing out of bounds.

The Raiders' supporters sat down again, and the Forty-Niners' fans had something to cheer. As the safety got up he ran past Dave, patting him on top of the helmet.

'Nice tackle, kid,' he said.

Again the San Francisco defense held out against the Oakland drive and the field goal attempt was blocked by Zal Yerkowicz, their big nose tackle. The rest of the players, on the bench, cheered the continued success of their special team.

Dave looked at Coach Haffkine, waiting for his call on their next play. But the man was fumbling in his pocket, taking out a small white envelope. Staring down at it, then holding it out to the English boy.

'Here. I was to give you this if you went on for your one play, Dave. Things haven't worked out that way so read it now.'

Dave took it off him, opening the flap of the envelope. Removing the small square of card. In a firm hand it said, simply: 'If you feel it's right, then do it. Good luck.' And it was signed: 'Joe Montana.'

Dave ran on, taking in another simple play. Simple, but one that depended totally on his own speed and agility in rolling out before making the pass. As the two teams lined up for the snap, he again caught the eye of Tommy Axler, who tried to throw him by winking and grinning.

'Not this time,' said Dave to himself, grinning back at the huge defensive end and throwing in a wink himself for good measure. Just for a sliver of frozen time, Dave was delighted to see a flicker of doubt behind the stone-solid composure of the Oakland player.

Inside his head, Dave was reeling off the stored pictures of Joe Montana at their training camp, showing him how to do it. Because of his poise and control when threatened with defeat, Joe was known as 'The Comeback Kid'. Twenty-four to fourteen with most of the third quarter and all of the fourth quarter left meant Dave had to emulate his hero in coming back.

'Ready, hut, hut, hut,' the ball hitting his hands on the third beat. The self-doubts were gone. So had the trembling in the knees. Now it was cool skill and control.

He faked the pass to the halfback, sending the Oakland defense the wrong way, rolled right, then planted his foot and pitched the ball to the long-legged Ben Michaels.

The sprinter caught it in open field position, outrunning the cover, striding in, head back, for a fabulous seventy-four yard touchdown.

Dave watched the ball sailing into Ben's hands, willing the American boy on, his own fists clenched with excitement. Jumping in the air as the touchdown was signalled. Schooling the broad grin off his face as he realised that the television camera was pointing in his direction. Wouldn't look good if he was gloating or showing off, he thought.

Ray Haffkine slapped him on the back as he came

off the field, and the rest of the team all clustered about him, shaking hands, Chip giving him the thumbs-up from where he sat with his ankle being strapped by the team's physio.

The kick was over and the gap had narrowed. Oakland now led by only twenty-four to twenty-one. And there was lots of time left.

Oakland's next series of possessions was held by the San Francisco defense, forcing them to punt when they failed to make the first down. Their kick landed on the fifty-two yard line of the Junior Forty-Niners team, being collected by Ben Michaels, who pushed back for a rapid twelve yard gain before he was tackled out of bounds.

After a quick first down pass to the tight end, Dave again tried the roll-out, eyes raking for a free receiver, spotting Tony Croft out on his own, neglected by the bewildered defense. Dave's agility and speed had bought him enough time to aim the football carefully, pitching it beyond the reach of a desperately leaping Oakland defender. Tony was able to take the pass and trot unopposed into the end zone for another touchdown.

Once again the extra point was good and the stunned home crowd had seen their team slip from being ten points ahead to four points down, all in the space of a couple of minutes. And this was with some unknown English kid playing as third-choice quarterback.

San Francisco now led by twenty-eight points to twenty-four.

★ ★ ★

For the Raiders, the agony continued. On their next drive, which took up most of the remainder of the third quarter, their quarterback threw an interception to the Forty-Niners strong safety, who ran four yards and then gave out a lateral pass to the only person on the team faster than Ben Michaels, their cornerback, Carl Meachum. He ran the football in a weaving pattern, clear to the Oakland twenty-two yard line.

Dave trotted on with Ray's instructions to put in two consecutive running plays. The first of them saw the clock run out, putting the big game into its final quarter.

Tommy Axler was striding around his defense, pushing and shouting at them, getting them fired up to resist the attack, successfully enough for both the running plays to get kicked back in their tracks for a net loss of four.

Dave took the signal for a deep pass left after a feint run to the right. Crouching, he called out the time for the snap.

The ball didn't come as clean as he liked, and he started to roll, but out of the corner of his eye he saw that the Mean Machine was up and lunging his way. Dave's mind was clicking like a computer on overtime. They were within field goal range. If he threw the ball he wouldn't get hit by Axler. But if he threw it, there was the chance of an interception.

It was no choice.

He tried to protect himself, hugging the ball in both arms, trying to roll as the huge black boy cannoned into him, sending him flying. But he kept hold on the ball.

Tommy Axler pulled him to his feet. 'Good play, my man,' he said. 'Take your bumps. But that's only the first. There'll be more.'

'I can't wait,' said Dave.

Ray Haffkine complimented him on his courage in taking the sack. The field goal was kicked, scraping over the crossbar. If Dave had been sacked further back, it would never have gone over.

The Forty-Niners inched further ahead by thirty-one points to twenty-four.

'They need a touchdown, just to draw level,' said Zal Yerkowicz.

Which seemed to Dave to be tempting providence a bit.

After the kick off to the Raiders, the skirmish became full-blooded war.

Fighting every inch of the way, the Oakland team clawed their way down the field in a series of drives, mixing runs and passes, each time just making the vital first down. But it ran the clock away. By the time they'd reached the Forty-Niners twelve yard line, there were barely four minutes remaining of the match.

It was third down and less than a yard to make. To the bewilderment of the Forty-Niners defense the Oakland short yardage back got the hand-off, and ran it laterally. Instead of dropping his head and bulldozing his way in, he looked up and threw a nine yard pass to the open tight end. Though he was smothered in tacklers, the boy battled his way from the two yard line, just managing to win the touchdown.

The extra kick brought the teams level again at thirty-one points each.

There were three minutes and fifty-five seconds remaining in the match.

'Keep your cool, Dave,' said Haffkine, sweat dripping off the end of his nose into his beard. He'd been running up and down the sideline for the whole game and looked more exhausted than any of the players. 'No mistakes. Keep it safe and careful.'

The San Francisco team regained possession of the football on their own seventeen yard line.

Dave felt great. In control, calm, knowing what plays would work, sticking to the safest percentage passes, never taking a risk when he didn't have to.

He generalled the drive, pushing and pushing at the Oakland defense. Tommy Axler was performing like the giant he was, but he still wasn't getting to Dave. During the drive, despite having the Mean Machine right up in his face, Dave got off a thirty-three yard pass to Tony Croft.

Ray Haffkine used one of their two remaining time-outs, calling Dave over. 'Three minutes and twenty to go. We're on their twenty-six yard line. A field goal can win it for us. But I'm goin' to leave that option right to the last. I want to beat them with a touch-down. Rub their noses in it more than a field goal ever can.'

'Sure.'

The Coach didn't even say anything this time about being careful. Dave appreciated that he was now

113

totally trusted. Joe Montana's message about if it felt right then do it came to him.

Another pass to Tony Croft brought them inside the ten. First and goal.

A running play that was blocked by the massive bulk of Axler.

Second and goal. Five yards only from the end-zone.

Another pass to a running back, who fought for a single yard.

Third and goal.

Oakland used up their penultimate time-out, trying to put pressure on Dave. Ray signalled for him to come again to the side of the field. The noise from the spectators was almost deafening and he had to shout to make himself heard. A skinny girl with a portable video camera on her shoulder came pushing forwards and Haffkine waved her away.

'Pass play, Dave. Stone double right. Don't let go unless . . . Heck, you know that, anyway. Don't worry. If we don't get in I'll send on the field-goal team.'

There were three minutes and four seconds showing on the big clock.

Dave looked along the bench at his team-mates. The pressure of holding the bigger Oakland squad was showing in the slumped shoulders and sagging mouths. Their kicker was warming up, face tense, licking his lips nervously. If the field goal was missed then the match looked set for overtime and a sudden death situation. Dave realised that Oakland were in better physical shape to cope with that.

He'd tucked the note in the pocket of his playing pants and he pulled it out, moments before running back on the pitch.

'If you feel it's right, then do it. Good luck. Joe Montana.'

'Yeah,' said Dave, to himself.

Third and goal on the Oakland four yard line. Dave called the pass play into the huddle, making sure everyone knew what should happen. At the last second he patted their full-back, Danny Blake, on the shoulder. 'If the receivers are covered, I might be behind you. Go for it.'

'Sure, Dave. Whatever you say, man.'

Crouching, the noise swelling around him. 'Hut, hut, hut,' taking the ball and rolling out on the third count, eyes covering the end-zone, looking for men clear. Noticing that Tommy Axler was bearing down towards him, clear of his block.

The pass play wasn't possible. But Danny Blake had done a great job, crashing over into the end-zone, leaving the narrowest of gaps in the Oakland defensive line. Dave made his decision.

He dug his heels in, powering himself forward, vaguely aware of yelling and screams from the crowd. Going for the gap, feeling Axler closing on him from the right.

A hand grabbed at his jersey, and someone flung themselves at his ankles. Then he was in the air, diving over the top of Danny, ball clamped in his arms.

Dave landed on his shoulder, starting to roll. A crushing weight crashed on top of him, knocking all the air from his lungs. He closed his eyes for a moment, opening them to see the face of Tommy Axler staring at him from between the bars of his helmet.

The next thing he saw was one of the officials, standing a yard away with both arms held vertically in the air. Signalling a . . .

'Touchdown!!!'

The yell came from thousands of throats, even from the supporters of the Raiders. The Mean Machine helped him up from the turf.

'Well done, kid.'

Then Dave was swamped by the rest of his team. Tony leaped in the air to slap hands in the high five, and Ray Haffkine was hugging him, beaming his delight.

The kick was good, giving the Junior Forty-Niners a lead of seven points, with two minutes and forty seconds on the clock.

The Raiders put all they had into a last effort, but Dave's unexpected touchdown had knocked the heart from them. They failed to convert a fourth down on their own forty-five line and the ball came back to Dave.

It was easy to hang on and run the clock down.

The last play of the match ended with Tommy Axler thundering in for the second sack of the afternoon against Dave, who still held on to the football. In the pandemonium, the tall black player shook him by the hand.

'You ever come back to California, then come guest

for us, not those Frisco bums,' he said, grinning broadly.

'You ever come to England, Tommy,' said Dave, 'I reckon we might just find a place for you with the Downham Destroyers.'

Dave woke around two in the morning, lying in his bed, staring into the dim light of the apartment. There had been great celebrations, hosted by Alix Cassady's father, where the toast had been, 'To the Limey with the good right arm. David Sheppard.'

Amidst the cheering and back-slapping, Ray Haffkine had given Dave a present.

In the darkness, Dave could just make it out, on top of a chest of drawers, by the window.

The football that he'd carried over for the winning touchdown.

Outside, in the San Francisco night, it was beginning to rain. Tomorrow, he would be home.

★★★★★★ The hand on his shoulder made him
11 jerk awake, looking around, unsure
for a moment where he was.
'Be landing in about half an hour.
★★★★★★ Thought you might like to see what
London looks like from the air.'

Dave grinned up at the TWA stewardess. 'Yeah.
Thanks a lot.'

'You're welcome.'

He'd slept most of the flight from New York's
Kennedy Airport, across the Atlantic. Uncle Don had
warned him that jet-lag would probably be worse
flying eastwards. It had been late afternoon when he'd
taken off from San Francisco, changing planes at New
York. His estimated time of arrival at Heathrow was
half past six in the morning.

The morning of Monday August 19th.

He looked out of the round window, still frosted
with ice from the high-altitude flight. Below him were
the small green fields of England, such a contrast to
the rolling brown mountains of the high Sierras that
he'd seen as his last glimpse of California. It was good
to be coming home.

His mind drifted back to his farewells to everyone
in San Francisco.

★ ★ ★

118

It seemed as if most of the San Francisco team had come along to see him off. Chip was there, still limping heavily, helped by Tony Croft and Mal Netzen. Ben Michaels was there, towering over Zal Yerkowicz. Ray Haffkine, with new ribbons plaited in his beard, wearing mirrored sunglasses, shouting and waving. Dave's hand grew sore from shaking so many times.

Eventually, Ray and Uncle Don shooed most of the boys away. Chip stayed with Tony. And Alix Cassady was there, demurely dressed in a loose blue denim shirt and stone-washed jeans. Her father was with her, still looking to Dave like a refugee from 'Dynasty'. But this time he didn't mention it.

'Good to meet you, Dave. Have a good flight and win some for us over there.'

'Thanks, Steve. You've been ever so kind. Everyone's been so kind.'

Ray Haffkine glanced across at Steve. 'You want to mention to Dave what we were talkin' about last night, after the partyin' was done?'

'You mean about the English team . . . No, let's mebbe leave it on the back burner a while. We said we'd talk to Don here 'bout it.'

Dave wondered what the air of mystery was all about. But it was driven from his mind by being grabbed from behind and having a big sloppy scented kiss planted on his cheek.

'You wouldn't go without saying goodbye to me, would you, honey?' shrilled Debby Altman, tottering along in the highest of heels and a Junior Forty-Niners playing shirt that was five sizes too tight for her.

At the last, when Dave and his uncle were about to go through the final barrier towards the plane, where Don would hand him to the stewardess, there were hurried farewells. In the end, only Chip, Alix and Ray came that far.

'So long, mate,' said Chip. 'You did real well, you know that. But I'm glad you're not staying here.'

'Why?' asked Dave.

'Because you'd get the job of starting quarterback and I kind of like it myself.'

The two boys laughed and shook hands.

Ray came next. 'I've said all the thanks there are, Dave. You were great. I've never seen a better display of courage and skill under pressure. Joe Montana would have been proud of you. Thanks for everything. Maybe we'll meet up again before too long.'

And last came Alix Cassady.

'If the Downham Destroyers ever need a cheer-leader,' she said, 'then just whistle. You do know how to whistle, don't you?'

'Course. Thanks for everything you and your Dad did. It was smashing of you. Bye.'

Dave stood there, grinning at the girl. For a hint of a moment he thought she was going to kiss him and he got ready to dodge it. At least, he thought he was getting ready to dodge it. But when she simply reached and shook his hand, there was an odd, empty feeling of disappointment.

A quick wave over his shoulder and he and Uncle Don were through the barrier and out of sight. Dave felt a wave of sadness sweep over him, eased by the knowledge that he was going home. Home to his family. But he'd had such good times.

'I've had such good times, Don,' he said. 'And please don't go all American and say "You're welcome". I couldn't bear it.'

'For sure,' replied his uncle.

'That's nearly as bad. But it's been fabulous. Better than anything I could ever have dreamed of. The city itself, the food, the Bay, Alcatraz, Muir Woods, ice-cream, the houses, the hills . . . Oh, everything.'

'And meeting Joe wasn't so bad, either.'

'No. And the game was all right, really.'

They both smiled at the memory.

It was only twenty-four hours since the winning touchdown, but it seemed like an eternity ago. Uncle Don looked at his watch. 'Got to go, Dave. You've made sure those two playing shirts are safe?'

'Yeah. I packed them in my case. Number ten for me and a number eighty-three as a present for Will. Ready for when we can *both* guest for the Junior Forty-Niners.'

'And the stuff for your family?'

'Yes.'

Dave had taken the easy and cheap way out. Each of his brothers and his sisters were getting a shake-up snow scene in a glass dome. The Golden Gate Bridge, Coit Tower, a grove of redwoods, Alcatraz and the TransAmerica pyramid building. He'd bought a spare one of Alcatraz to give to Wilburn's parents.

For his own parents he'd agonised for ages. His first thought had been to buy them each a tee-shirt that said: 'My Son Went All The Way To San Francisco And All He Bought Me Was This Lousy Tee-Shirt', but he decided that it was too corny.

In the end he'd settled on a book about San Francisco, with lovely colour photographs, that had been marked down to a price he could afford. He thought it might give his own memories more substance as well. There were also going to be Chip's photos to look forward to and Ray Haffkine had promised him cuttings from the papers about the match. Uncle Don had said he'd do what he could with the local TV station to get a video that he could send to England.

'This is it, sport,' said his uncle. 'Been great having you. I'll be back in England in time for Christmas. With any luck we can all stay up and watch the Superbowl together again.'

'It's a date,' said Dave.

'This is your captain speaking. We'll be landing in about fifteen minutes at London Heathrow, where the time is six ten in the morning, and the temperature is fifty-four degrees. Ground control tell me that it's raining, but the forecast is for it to clear giving a fine, sunny day.'

'You're so brown!'
    'Put on a bit of weight.'
    'How was Don?'
    'Good flight?'
    'We got your cards.'
    'Did you sleep on the plane?'

'Came in early.'

'No problems with customs?'

'You're so brown, Dave.'

The sleep on the flight made Dave feel in better shape than he'd expected. It was great to see his parents, leaning out of the crowd at the terminal, his mother waving to him. Next to her a man in a dark uniform was holding a torn piece of brown cardboard that said, 'Meeting Mr Aziz Patel from Karachi.'

All the way home on the Underground, through the waking city, they bombarded him with questions. The news of the meeting with Joe Montana and his success in the big match was greeted with great delight by both of them.

Though, in a quiet moment, Dave was aware that he could never properly convey to them how wonderful it had been. Or even how well he'd played. Or how important it had been to so many people. And he felt a bit sorry about that.

Dad had parked the car at Bishop's Stortford station, ready to drive them home. It seemed chilly and Dave pulled on his anorak. The roads looked narrow and cramped after the freeways around San Francisco. He tried to keep up with all their questions, avoiding any mention of Alix Cassady. Knowing that his dad would start teasing him about her.

Knowing as well that there wasn't anything for him to be teased about.

★ ★ ★

All the family were there, filling the house, when he got back and there was a big banner across the front door, saying 'Welcome Home, Dave'. He handed out the presents, stolidly facing up to everyone telling him how sun-tanned and brown he looked. And how the weather in England had been rotten while he'd been away.

Sunday lunch was one of his favourites. Lamb with mint sauce and roasties, followed by chocolate steamed pudding and custard. He didn't honestly feel all that hungry, but he could see how bitterly disappointed his mother would be if he didn't eat plenty.

'Suppose you want to go round and see Will, tell him all about the States?' said Dad, as they sat in the familiar living-room, the papers strewn all round the floor.

'Yes, please. Is that all right?'

'Course,' replied Mum. 'But don't stay too long. You want to get to bed good and early.'

'Uncle Don says that with jet-lag you have to try and stay up on your first night home until around your usual bed-time.'

'Aren't you tired, love?' asked his mother, peering at him worriedly.

'Not too bad. Honest.'

'Well, come back by about five. I'm doin' egg and chips for supper.'

'All right. And thanks for the dinner, Mum. It's nice to get back to English food.'

He waited a second, suddenly realising with a shock that he was waiting for his mother to smile sweetly and say: 'You're welcome.'

It *was* good to be home.

★ ★ ★

The rain had eased, leaving only a fine drizzle that cooled his face as he walked around the corner to Wilburn's house. He felt strange.

It didn't seem right that everything was still the same as when he went.

He somehow thought there ought to be changes. New houses built or different neighbours. But it was like it always was. It felt just like a normal summer afternoon in Eastbury.

Dave rang the bell on the front door of number nine, Sundial Grove. He heard scurrying feet in the hall. The door was opened by Wilburn's little brother, Errol.

'Hello, Dave. You aren't half sunburned,' he squeaked.

Mr and Mrs Thomas both smiled to see him back safely and they admired their souvenir of Alcatraz, hidden in a violent snowstorm when you shook the glass globe. Will leaned over the banisters, calling for him to come up to his bedroom.

Just for a minute there was a slight unease between them, as if they both worried the other might have changed. But it quickly passed. Wilburn had a plate of biscuits and a couple of cans of Coke in his room, and he poured one out for Dave.

'Did you drink a lot of this?' was his first question.

'Yeah.'

Will sat down on his bed and Dave took his usual place in an old armchair in the corner of the room, by the speakers of his friend's music centre.

'Any news around here?' asked Dave.

Will shook his head. 'Not really. Car knocked down

the wall at the far end of Natal Street. Been rainin' a lot.'

'Oh, yeah. Mum 'n Dad said that.'

'Come on, then,' said Will.

'Got you a present,' holding out the plastic bag from one of the souvenir stores down on Fisherman's Wharf.

'Hey, it's great. What team is it?'

'Junior San Francisco Forty-Niners.'

'You play for 'em? Hey, did you meet Joe Montana and get his autograph and all that?'

Dave thought of the smudged square of card that now rested on his mantelpiece back home. 'Yeah. I'll show you when you come round.'

'Honest? Wow! Come on, mate. I want to hear all about it, right from the start. Was it a rave, Dave?'

'It was brill, Will. Really brill.'

'Well . . .?'

'First thing I remember is wakin' up on the plane over San Francisco. My stomach gave a lurch . . . . .'